I Love You More Than Love

TERRI SEYMORE-GREEN

I LOVE YOU MORE THAN LOVE

TERRI SEYMORE-GREEN

Published by Poetry & Prose Publishing, LLC

PUBLISHER'S NOTE

This is a work of fiction. Names, characters, places, and incidents either are a product of the author's imagination or are used fictitiously, and any resemblance to actual persons, living or dead, business establishments, events, or locales is entirely coincidental.

Book cover designed by JD&J with stock imagery provided by [michael jung] © 123RF.com

ISBN: 0692876626
ISBN-13: 978-0692876626

I LOVE YOU MORE THAN LOVE

DEDICATION

To my sons, Brandon and Derreck. Thank you for all the love
and support you have given me throughout this process.
You have always been my biggest inspirations.
I love you both dearly.

To every woman who has experienced a "Darius" in her
lifetime. This is also for you.

CONTENTS

ACKNOWLEDGMENTS

First and foremost, I want to thank my Heavenly Father for helping me to identify my true gifts and talents, and for showing me how to let my faith be bigger than my fears.

Brandon and Derreck, you two have always been in my corner, giving me praise along the way. I thank you for your consistent encouragement, love, support, and laughter. There were times when I thought I would pull every strand of my hair out when things weren't going as planned, but you helped me to find something positive in it. To my sister, Allison. I thank you for being who you are. No one could ever fill your shoes. Thank you for getting the word out there to friends, family, strangers, and anyone else who would listen. I thank my parents, Samuel and Patricia for giving me life. It is because of you that I am able to do what I do. Jeramy, all I can say is wow! You have sacrificed so much for me, and I thank you for it.

Michael Baisden, we've only met once many years ago but you offered me some valuable advice. You told me that I would have to get rid of those people in my life who couldn't support my dreams. I did eventually listen, and life has been better ever since.

Finally, I would be remiss if I didn't mention the one person who was there when this all began. Shelton, thank you for encouraging me to write this story.

1 KEISHA

I arrived home from work a little later than normal. Traffic in the DC area was a nightmare and very unpredictable. Kicking off my four and a half inch pumps, I headed to my home office to grab my laptop from the desk. I was so exhausted, but I hadn't checked my e-mail in about four days because I was so busy trying to finish the monthly report for my branch. Management positions in the banking and finance industry sometimes meant putting in late hours at the office and from the comfort of my home. So, I was going to have to find time to go through my personal email after I took my shower. I plugged in my computer and powered it up before heading into the bathroom to get the water nice and hot like I liked it. I logged onto my e-mail to preview whether there was anything important hidden amongst the junk mail that I always just automatically deleted. Already, I had missed a sale at Macy's and my last chance to get lace panties five for $25 at Victoria's Secret. There were actually three of those in the past three days, so I hadn't missed much. I deleted them, but decided to keep the one from MAC. I knew I needed to check out some of the new winter colors to update my makeup kit. I had an upcoming wedding event and was expected to make the bride and her bridal party beautiful; and MAC would probably have some great new colors I could try out on them.

I had been freelancing as a Make-Up Artist for over a year now and although it was a lucrative side job that I absolutely loved doing, I still needed gainful and steady employment; and most importantly, medical benefits. Just this past spring and summer alone, I had twelve weddings, six proms, and a handful of graduates who wanted to look their absolute best in photos that would preserve the memories forever. Though some seasons weren't as busy as others, you could always count on spring and summer. Over all, I was doing quite well between my career at the bank and my new-found business venture, so I had no complaints.

Suddenly, an e-mail address caught my attention. DKinston2@yahoo.com. I hadn't seen this one in a while. It had been at least six months since I had even received a phone call from Darius because I changed my phone numbers. After changing both the cell and landline numbers, he began calling my job which was unacceptable, not to mention a little disrespectful considering he had been told not to call me ever again. After about a month, he was tired of me hanging up on him so he stopped calling. Now, here he was reaching out in the only remaining way that he knew he could; through email.

Not sure how I would handle this situation, I decided to wash the events of the day out of my mind and off my body in the shower that was now steaming up the bathroom mirrors. Would I read what he had to say, or just delete it? I toyed around with the idea of reading it, but what if I regretted doing it after? It would be too late.

I lathered my Coconut Miracle Oil body wash all over my body, let the hot water run down my back for at least ten minutes, dried myself off and headed back to the bed. I couldn't help but wonder what Darius wanted. My mind wandered back to the end of our relationship. He had gotten a little crazy when I told him not to contact me anymore and when he refused to do so; I cut off every means of communication that he'd known. Or at least I thought I had. Darius and I had dated for only a short while, but the time we spent together over our eight or nine-month relationship was primarily good. We were inseparable from the first day we met until the day we parted ways, so it was a little difficult to get used to being without him. Now, here he was trying to reach out.

In my mind, I thought about other men I'd dated. There hadn't been that many, but of the few; Darius was the one who held the dearest place in my heart even though we were no longer together. He was the one that set my soul on fire when he touched me. He was the most sincere and cared about how I was doing without me ever having to question what his motive was. He just wanted to love me, but Darius had a major flaw that I couldn't live with. It was wreaking havoc on our relationship, so I had to let it go.

2 HOW IT ALL BEGAN

It was a Saturday afternoon and I was hosting a dinner party at Jamel's house. Jamel and I had met in college during our freshman year. He was seeking a bachelor's degree in Marketing and I was majoring in Finance. We remained close friends after graduation, but eventually went our separate ways. Although we never dated, there was a short time of attraction between us. I'm not sure what it was for him, but for me, it was his long dreadlocks. They made him look so sexy. That, coupled with the way he dressed, his politeness, and intelligence made him seem like the perfect catch; but we never crossed the line and just kept it friendly. There were times I'd thought about trying to hook him up with one of my girlfriends, but just never got around to it. There were only a couple who would even be worthy of a man like Jamel. He was the perfect gentleman. The kind of guy who always opened doors for you, never let you pay for anything, held an umbrella over your head in the rain even though it poured down on him. He would stop to help change a stranger's tire . . . that type stuff.

Anyway, after college, he ended up in New York and I ended up in Washington, DC. After several years of maintaining our friendship with 230 miles between us, we both ended up buying homes in Maryland not far from each other, and the rest is history. We lived about ten minutes apart and saw each other at least two or three times a week for dinner, a movie, or just to talk; but we spoke on the phone or sent text messages back and forth almost every day.

Jamel and I shared a lot of mutual friends who would be joining us for dinner at his house at 6:00. In fact, I was preparing all the food. I suppose I inherited my cooking talents from my dad. He was actually a better cook than my mom, but I would never say that in front of her. Mom's specialties included spaghetti, fried chicken, and macaroni and cheese; regular every day stuff. But my dad? He was a gourmet style chef. He'd actually worked at a five-star restaurant part-time when I was a child because he wanted my mom to be able to stay home and raise me. He did whatever he had to do to make that happen, which meant working two jobs.

Jamel and our crew had eaten many a meal at my house, so when he asked me to be in charge of tonight's menu for his event, of course I agreed. There wasn't a whole lot that I wouldn't do for him. I'd check on his place when he was out of town, run interference when he was trying to get out of a bad date, and remind him of special events and anniversaries. I even went as far as to order flowers for his mother on her birthday, or for his sister when she gave birth to his nephew. The truth is, he would do similar things for me, so our relationship was definitely full of give and take. I loved that dude like he was of my own flesh and blood.

Anyway, I had decided at the last minute to bake a coconut cake that evening. Jamel requested curried chicken, rice and peas and curried cabbage for dinner and a coconut cake would really be a great ending to a delicious meal. Unfortunately, I didn't have half the necessary ingredients and barely had time to pull it all together; but I would.

I had to make a run to the local Food Lion to get the ingredients for the cake, so I threw on my Nikes and headed out the door. I was really pressed for time, but found everything I needed in a matter of minutes. As I began putting my items on the checkout lane store conveyor belt, there he was. He must have been about 6'2 with the waviest jet black hair. He looked in my direction with the most beautiful brown eyes I'd ever seen. People had often told me how beautiful my brown eyes were, but mine were nothing compared to his. They were so light, you could almost see through them. I was in a daze from the second I looked at him.

We exchanged glances and smiles as he passed me by and headed down aisle four with a little boy who looked to be about ten or eleven years old. I assumed he was his son, because he had been blessed with the same features; down to the jet black wavy hair.

"That'll be $24.56," said the cashier reaching for my Visa debit card.

My eyes followed the back of Mr. handsome as he threw a bag of potato chips into his cart. I'd frequented this grocery store several times a week, but had never been graced with his presence before.

"Miss?" the young lady interrupted my thoughts.

"Oh, I'm sorry," I apologized and released my grip on the card, all the while hoping she would take her time completing the transaction. I needed to see those brown eyes again.

As I looked down at my t-shirt, I wanted to kick

myself. There were small specks of curry sauce spattered across the front, and I hadn't put on lipstick, earrings, or anything before racing out of the house. That was so out of character for me. I remember my mother always telling me to make sure whenever I went out that I went appropriately because you never knew who you might run into. Years of grooming for fashion shows and go-sees during my modeling years had paid off up until this very moment. My mother would have been quite embarrassed to see me right now, but it was too late. The man of my dreams had already seen me at my worst and there was nothing I could do about it. I made a mental note to never let it happen again as I headed into the parking lot with my bags in tow.

"Excuse me, Miss. Do you need me to help you with those bags?" said a voice from behind immediately catching my attention.

There he was, standing there pushing an empty grocery cart in my direction. Flattered, I smiled and placed the three bags into the cart and continued walking in the direction of my car. *I should have listened to my mother.*

"A lady as fine as you should never have to carry her own bags," he said. "My first name's Darius. Do you mind if I ask you yours Mrs. Kingston?"

"Excuse me? I think you must have me mixed up with someone else," I admitted.

"No, no confusion. Kingston is my last name. I just need to know your first."

"Cute," I blushed. "My name is Keisha. My last name is Johnston. That's the first time I've ever heard that one. Well, Boys II Men actually used it first in one of their songs, I think."

"No, I've never used it before," he promised, reaching in his pocket for his cell phone. "I saw you and I knew I had finally seen the woman I've been dreaming about since I was fifteen years old."

"I told my son we were going to stop here to pick up some sodas and snacks for our fishing trip, and there you were. So, where are you rushing off to?" he asked, placing the bags into the trunk of my car.

"I'm trying to get back home. I'm cooking for a friend's dinner party tonight and I needed a few last minute things," I said as I looked into his eyes one last time. "I appreciate your help," I smiled, reaching for the door handle of my new BMW.

"Before you race off, what do you like to do in your free time?" he asked, blocking my car door so that I couldn't get away without answering his question.

"I don't know. I like going to the movies, reading, listening to music, shopping like most women, I guess. I stay pretty busy between my day job and a side gig I've been doing for a while now."

He sure was good looking. I couldn't help but admire his caramel colored skin and very well groomed goatee. He was sporting a chin strap that looked like he'd just left the barber's chair before heading to the store. He was sexier than any man I'd ever laid eyes on. I mean that literally. Remembering that I was standing in the Food Lion parking lot with no make-up on my face, my hair pulled back in a tight bun, in jeans and sneakers with a white t-shirt stained with curry sauce, my face became flushed with embarrassment.

"There's this new jazz place that just opened not too far from here; Gee's Spot. Have you ever heard of it?"

"Yeah, in fact I have heard of it. My girlfriend's brother owns it," I admitted. "I haven't been there yet, though."

"I was wondering if you'd be interested in listening to some music and enjoying a meal with me sometime in the near future," he asked very innocently. "I'd love to take you there."

"Yes, I'd like that," I admitted, reaching for a pen so that

I could give him my number.

"Girl, don't you know we're in the technology age? Here, let me program it in my cell phone right now. I definitely don't want to lose it," he admitted, pulling up a new page in his address book.

"You ready?" I asked. "It's 301-555-0093."

"Great. Do you mind if I give you mine as well?" he asked, confident that I would take it. "I just dialed your number. Please program it in as soon as possible. I wouldn't want you to forget who it belongs to. Remember, Darius. D-A-R-I-U-S."

This guy was smooth, but there was no way I was going to forget who that number belonged to. I'd also remember how attractive he was, those beautiful brown eyes, and his swag if I remembered nothing else. Besides, he'd already gotten me to commit to going to Gee's spot, and giving up the digits in a matter of minutes. Any other time I'd be trying to get the number so that I wouldn't have to give mine out. I liked to stay in control of who called and when they called. If he turned out not to be my type, I just wouldn't call again. My usual plan had just gone out the window. There was something different about this one. So, I had broken my own rule.

"By the way, where's your son?" I asked, standing in the doorway to my vehicle.

"DJ? He's waiting for me in the store," he laughed, pointing toward the large storefront window where his son was posted with a big smile on his face.

DJ just stood there watching the entire exchange, but never came out of the store to interrupt our conversation. He was just as handsome as his father, and a little gentleman. I waved in his direction before getting into the car and closing the door. He waved back. Darius ran back toward the store, turning to wave good-bye with a sexy wink from those brown eyes before going back inside. From that day forward, I had visions of him in my dreams. I looked forward to seeing him again.

3 DARIUS & KEISHA

I dried my body very quickly because I was anxious to read the message from Darius. What did he have to say after all these months? Why all of a sudden? My nerves began to get the best of me. I wanted to know, but then again, I didn't. After slipping into an oversized t-shirt, I stretched out on my bed with my laptop; clicking on the message with the subject line, "I hope you're okay".

Keisha,

I've been thinking about you daily and was a little disappointed to find out that you had changed your numbers, although I understand why you did. I know I took you through a lot and for that, I am truly sorry. I miss hearing your voice and seeing your beautiful face. I miss your laughter, and your smile; but most of all I miss holding you in my arms. If you can find the time, please give me a call. My number hasn't changed. No pressure. I just want to see how things are going. You know I'll always love you no matter what. I love you more than . . . love.

Darius

He really knew how to get to me. Our relationship had been like riding on a roller coaster. It was up and down from one day to the next, although we never fought and rarely ever argued about anything. We had spent every single day together from the first date until he moved to Atlanta to follow his career. We found ourselves in very intimate positions at least once a day and sometimes two or three times. He was by far the best man I had ever dated, and I missed his touch like wilted flowers missed the water needed to sustain them.

I had briefly gotten involved with someone else after we broke up, but there was not a man alive who could make me feel the way Darius did. The way he touched me was electric and the things he said would make my body feel so warm inside that we would be innocently watching television, then suddenly entangled in each other's arms on his living room floor or any place that we wanted to. No matter where the urge hit us, it became our place, and although I had grown up in a Christian family and knew that it was wrong; I still did it. In his shower, on his balcony; even in his pool. You get the picture. I'll spare you the details. But I must say, if you name any place, you best believe our bodies were familiar with it and it was from that day forward; marked as our territory. Darius had me doing things I never thought I'd ever do, but with him I was able to free my inhibitions and again, I knew it was wrong; but I found it difficult to resist him. I had always been self-conscious in my nakedness, but to him I was the most beautiful woman in the world. We were addicted to each other.

I hit the reply button to begin my response to the man who still had a special place in my heart although we were no longer together. I wanted things to be different between us. Yes, I missed him but I also remembered why and how the relationship ended.

Hi Darius,

It's really nice to hear from you. I apologize for the late response, but I haven't checked my e-mail in a few days. I hope all is well with you and DJ. Please give him my love. A lot has happened on my end and I hope that I'll be able to bring myself to share it with you someday . . .

Keisha

I hesitated before hitting the send button and decided to dial his number instead.

"Hello?" he said, answering after the third ring.

"Hey, Darius, how are you?" I asked. "It's me, Keish," using the nickname he'd given to me while we were dating.

"Who is this?" he asked confusingly.

"It's your ex! So, you've already forgotten about me, huh?" I joked.

"Oh, Keisha! Girl, how in the heck have you been?" he asked.

There was a moment of silence as I wasn't sure what to say. We hadn't spoken in almost six months, so I was a little uncomfortable. After all, we had parted ways on bad terms and although he'd sent an occasional e-mail or text message to my cell phone, after he pissed me off we never spoke over the phone again. It was just too painful for both of us. He spent so much energy trying to convince me to give the relationship another try that I became emotionally

21

exhausted, and detached myself from the situation. I went as far as to disconnect myself from all of my feelings for him. I knew it would drive him crazy, but the constant phone calls and messages were overwhelming. Once it became too much to take, I ended all communication with him, but I forgot about the e-mail address that he had access to. The truth is, I rarely ever used it and didn't really think getting rid of it was necessary at the time.

When we had the argument that ended things, he had already transferred to the airport in Atlanta to assume his duties as Air Traffic Controller. He had been drinking way too much. I was constantly nagging him about getting help for his habit. He didn't think he had a problem, we argued, he hung up the phone and that was it. The stubborn part of me wouldn't allow me to call him back after he hung up. It was almost as if I was released from the burden of having to take care of an alcoholic. A couple of weeks went by before either of us picked up the phone to call the other. If I remember correctly, he made the first move. I was still so angry with him about the last conversation that I really wasn't trying to hear what he had to say. I knew I was not going to be the shoulder to hold him up ever again because he was too intoxicated to walk. I know love is supposed to be unconditional, but in nine months, Darius had sucked the life out of me with his drinking. Yet, I was still in love. If he had agreed to get help back then, I would have stuck it out with him. Ride or die. But he couldn't admit he had a problem. So, I had to let go of our toxic relationship.

"Oh, my God, it's so good to hear your voice. Baby, how've you been?" he asked. "I've been thinking about you so much!"

"I've been okay," I said, trying not to offer too much more information before determining what direction the conversation was headed in.

"Only okay?" he asked trying to see if I was currently seeing anyone. I knew him so well.

"Just work, work and more work," I said.

"Well, you know what they say about all of that work. All work and no play is no fun at the end of the day," he said in the sexy voice that I remembered.

"How's DJ?"

"His football team won a championship and he's doing very well in school. I'm no longer working in Atlanta. I took a position at Dulles International Airport. I needed to get back home."

Without all the details, I concluded that he had been to hell and back just like I had. Don't get me wrong, I was doing very well in my career. Financially, I was doing extremely well. I was getting ready to move into a new home, had just upgraded my 5 series BMW to a 750LI and was looking and feeling better than I'd felt in a very long time. I hadn't had a Sickle Cell crisis in five months and my recent blood work was excellent. God had given me the opportunity to visit a couple of places that I'd never been before. I'd traveled to St. Thomas, St. Maarten, and the Bahamas as well as Las Vegas in the short time since we had broken up. I had never been to either of those places and was convinced that I needed to go someplace I'd never been at least twice a year. More than that if circumstances allowed for it.

Life overall was good, but my personal life sucked. I hadn't experienced love the way I had with him and although I'd dated, I just couldn't find happiness. No one could love on me the way Darius did. He was so attentive to my every physical, emotional and mental need. I really believed he was my soulmate.

Our friends all wondered why we broke up. Well, here goes. Darius had some major issues that he needed to get worked out before he would be able to give one hundred percent to any relationship. His most serious issue was the alcoholism. I felt bad for leaving him at a time when he needed me more than ever, but I grew up with two parents who suffered from alcoholism. When my father was drinking heavily, it was nothing for him to strike my mom or scare her so badly that she would grab me and lock the two of us in a room. By the grace of God, they had both been delivered years ago of their illnesses. Through counseling, lots of prayer, and a relationship with God, they were both doing well. In fact, they were living faithfully in the church and were both enjoying the retired life. Even though things were good now, I just couldn't suffer through any more than I had as a child, and it was too hard to watch Darius put DJ through it. It wasn't fair for that little boy to have to take care of his father who was too drunk to take care of himself most of the time.

"No, I'm doing great; really. But you're so right. I probably work too much. I suppose I haven't been getting out as much as I used to, but I still enjoy spending time with the girls when I'm not at home."

"Baby, I really need to see you. There is so much I have to tell you," he confessed.

"Darius, I don't know if I can do that right now," admitting I wasn't ready. My heart really wanted to see him, but my mind wouldn't let me forget the past.

"Baby, listen. I know I put you through so much when we were together, but if you'll just agree to see me I promise you won't be disappointed. There's so much I would like to tell you, but I have to do it in person. Over the phone just won't do. I'm not trying to put any pressure on you, but I've been miserable without you. Please, just meet me for dinner or a cup of coffee or something. I promise I won't do anything to upset you. I just need to see you," he admitted.

"Sweetie, just let me think about it," I begged, trying to

change the subject. Had I just called him Sweetie?

"So, how's work?"

I was in no way ready to see him, because I knew if I agreed, we would probably end up in bed. We were so physically and emotionally connected to one another that each time we saw each other, we ended up in each other's arms at the least. I hadn't been intimate with anyone in several months. The brief relationship that followed the break up didn't last because we were just not compatible in any way, and compatibility is important. Some people believe that opposites attract. I believe that too, but it has never worked out for me beyond the initial attraction. The rebound guy wasn't even affectionate or caring. He was nothing like Darius. Let's face it; no one would ever measure up to him. If he hadn't been a heavy drinker, we would still be together. Maybe even engaged and living together or something.

The reality is that I knew I wasn't strong enough to be alone with him just yet. The mere thought of him sent my imagination wandering through one of our intimate encounters from the past. If my parents knew what I had been up to, they would have disapproved and I'm a grown woman, but I still cared so much about what they thought about me. Still, I wanted something that I knew I didn't need.

"I'll really think about it, but I can't give you an answer right at this moment. I hope you understand," I said.

Even if he didn't, my answer would have to do for now.

"Okay, baby. I said no pressure and I meant it," he surrendered. "Can I call you tomorrow? It's getting late, and I know you have to get up very early in the morning."

He was always so considerate. Maybe I was crazy, because he possessed so many qualities that a lot of women I knew were looking for. There were even a few who tried to snatch him up when I first met him. They would subtly make flirtatious remarks, and would show up at events they knew we would be attending, looking like a million bucks. Luckily, I was confident and secure in our relationship, so it never bothered me. Darius was the epitome of the perfect man when you looked at him. He was charismatic, had a beautiful smile, was a good talker, and always looked as handsome as he could; but I knew some of his deepest, darkest secrets. I probably put up with him longer than some others might have, but I truly loved him and thought I could change him. Although in reality, I knew I couldn't. I had so many things I was trying to accomplish that I was afraid to open the door to spending even a little bit of my time with him. He would definitely be a distraction. He always had been, but I don't mean that in a bad way. I just kept thinking about spending every single day with him for the entire nine months we dated. Every single day. That's a lot of time for two people who weren't even married. I was burned out. I felt like I was losing myself . . . my identity. I felt convicted in my spirit because I knew that I hadn't been raised to behave like that.

I remember him trying to convince me to sell my house and move in with him. He wanted me to be with him every waking moment.

"Keisha, we're spending all of our time either at my place or at yours. Think about how much money we're throwing away by paying two mortgages," he said.

There was no way I was going to give up my house when I was already struggling to hold onto the relationship with all of the drunken episodes I had to endure. Though I had to admit, in the back of my mind, I did miss him. I missed the laughter, the gentle touches, our conversations, and doing things with him that I would never consider doing with anyone else. Maybe I was crazy for not agreeing to meet with him? No, not crazy; just confused. I didn't know what to do, but I believed time would reveal it. I did know that I didn't want to make a decision in haste. I really needed to think about it.

"Darius, let me sleep on it if you don't mind," I almost begged. "Is it okay if I give you a call in the morning? Say around 10:00? I should be done with my work out by then." I said, waiting for his response.

"Yes, 10:00 o'clock sounds good. I'll talk to you in the morning. I love you."

"I love you too," I confessed, looking at my cell phone display before hanging up. I really did love him.

Going back to the email message he'd sent, I clicked on the link to a Joe song. The lyrics to "If You Lose Her" began to play. As I listened to the words, it was as if Joe had been eavesdropping on our relationship. The song said everything I'd been feeling during our time spent together and what lead to our end. Apparently, Joe knew how Darius and I both felt. I listened intently through to the end of the song, and listened again. Immediately, I felt a desire to see him. I knew at that moment I would agree to meet him for dinner. Maybe he had changed? I would never know unless I gave him an opportunity to at least say what was on his mind. Besides, I would want someone to give me the same courtesy. I guess tomorrow he would get his chance. Before going to bed, I downloaded the rest of the songs from Joe's CD so I could listen while trying to fall asleep. I knew it wouldn't be easy because Darius was now on my mind, and I couldn't shake the thoughts.

4 DARIUS

I was having a hard time trying to contain myself waiting for Keisha to call. I really didn't think she would ever call me back after some of the things I put her through. Don't get me wrong, I treated her like a lady throughout our entire relationship. As long as I was sober, that is. The problems began just a week before I was scheduled to leave town for Atlanta, or at least so I thought. Some of my family members had thrown a going away party on my behalf. I had a little too much to drink. Okay, I had way too much to drink and passed out. This was something that Keisha had become accustomed to while dating me. I wouldn't admit it then, but I was an alcoholic. There wasn't a day that I didn't partake in some sort of alcohol. From the mild stuff to the hard core. I had to have it. My system had come to rely on it, and before I knew it I couldn't function without it. To me, during that time it was more important than eating. My meals were mostly of a liquid nature and filled with alcohol.

The night of the party, I remember throwing back one after another, alternating shots with bottles of beer. Things were going good at first. We were dancing, laughing, and having a great time. My cousins wanted to get a card game going and Keisha and I were winning. That is until I passed out right in the middle of the game. According to some of my cousins, there I sat with my head hung low like the mossy oak trees lining the streets of some of the oldest plantations in the deepest parts of the south. Just leaning.

My family was used to seeing me that way. It had become a regular routine for them to have to carry me out of this event or that one. With the help of my cousins, Stacey and Steve, Keisha had to literally carry me to the car. There we were an hour away from home and she had to drive us back to her place because I was so drunk, I'd passed out.

Once we made it back to the house, it took Keisha more than 30 minutes to get me out of the car. There she was, trying to wake DJ up who was sleeping soundly in the back seat. She wanted to get him into the house first, so he wouldn't have to witness yet, another drunken episode. Then with all of her strength, she dragged me out of the car the best way she could in the pouring rain. She went to bed very upset and angry that night. It was the first night since we started dating that we had not been intimate. She was mad and left me asleep on the living room floor, drunk out of my mind.

Things were tense after that. The following week, I was headed to Atlanta. The original plan was for Keisha to transfer down after she could sell her house and secure a transfer with her company. But once I arrived in Atlanta, our conversations were few and far between, and when we did talk she was very short with me.

I didn't want to admit it, but we were nearing the end.

Keisha had finally been freed of the responsibility of dealing with an alcoholic. A few weeks later, things sort of fizzled out. I'm sure me telling her that I was headed to the strip club with some friends from work for happy hour sealed our fate. I don't know what I was thinking. I knew she was over it, and instead of trying to talk to her when she became upset; I hung up on her.

In my mind, I couldn't understand why she would get so upset about an innocent evening out with the fellas, but she did. In reality, Keisha was also concerned with the career path I'd chosen and how being an alcoholic just didn't go with it. She worried about the lives that I could have put in jeopardy by showing up for work drunk, although I never did that. I was a functional alcoholic when it came to my career. The truth is, I took her for granted. I really believed she would call me back, but she didn't. Keisha wasn't one to put up with a bunch of drama and she was at her limit with me. Several months passed, and there were no phone calls, text messages, or emails. The silence was killing me, so I did the only thing I knew how to do; I got wasted.

Finally, after a month or so I got up enough courage to call her, but things were different and after three days there was no communication. I had to face the fact that I had totally screwed it all up. I lost the one woman who I knew could complete my life, and it hurt like nothing I'd ever felt before. I felt like I was living in hell. The ache I felt in my heart was worse than the loss of a loved one. It felt like I was in my darkest hour. As I stood there on the balcony of my condo overlooking downtown Atlanta, I began to cry. Yes, a grown man crying over a woman. I know for certain the liquor had fueled what I was feeling. I missed her so much. I knew I had to make some changes if she was going to take me seriously ever again. So, at that moment, I decided to stop drinking.

After getting myself together, I went into the kitchen

and poured out every ounce of alcohol I had in the house. I took the empty bottles down to the recycling bin because I didn't want the scent of alcohol being anywhere near me. The temptation would be too great, but I needed my woman back more than I needed the liquor. Let me be clear about one thing. My decision to stop drinking was not because of my love for Keisha, it was because I loved myself more than I had ever shown her. I needed to love myself before I could truly love her the way she deserved to be loved.

A couple months into my sobriety, I found out that Dulles International Airport in Northern, Virginia had an open position. It was settled. I was leaving Hartsfield-Jackson Atlanta International for Washington-Dulles International Airport as soon as possible. I needed to get my baby back. I e-mailed her to let her know I was coming home, but there was no response. I decided to give her a call, but she didn't want to see me and I was devastated. Eventually, she changed her number. I didn't even get the chance to tell her I was sober and was attending Alcoholics Anonymous and counseling sessions several days a week. Not only did my career depend on this, but my life did too. Yet and still, Keisha wouldn't give me the chance to explain. The fact that my calls went unanswered wasn't going to stop me from trying to get her back. She was the woman I wanted to spend the rest of my life with, and I would do anything to prove it to her.

Over the next few weeks, I spent countless nights getting minimal sleep because I couldn't stop thinking about her, wondering what she was doing, or if she was even thinking about me at all. I remember asking God to please send her back, down on my knees praying like I'd never prayed before. I had never cried for a woman in my entire life; but I shed tears over her and I didn't care who knew.

During the whole ordeal, my family feared I was

emotionally unstable. I remember my mother saying that I was mourning like Keisha had died. That's what it felt like to me, and I didn't like it. My cousins called me a punk and said I needed to man up. That's the mild version of what they really said. I was losing control. The man I saw in the mirror wasn't anyone I knew. He was just a shell of the man I used to be with very little resemblance to the strong, black man everyone else loved and respected. I was broken. Keisha had really done a number on me.

Thinking back, the strangest thing about all of this is that it wasn't about the sex. In many of my past relationships, it had always been about the sex. In fact, that was all it was about. I didn't care about any one of them, but this one? She was the one. Now, the sex was better than any I'd ever had, but it was the way I felt when I was with her that made all the difference in the world. Just to be in her presence was like walking in heaven. The way she held my hand and looked into my eyes with that beautiful smile and those deep dimpled cheeks melted my heart every time. Keisha completed me. She was my soulmate. She still is.

My cell phone rang at 9:59. She was always prompt. I felt beads of sweat on my forehead as I hit the call button on my vehicle's Bluetooth system.

"Hey, Baby," I said, wiping my forehead with a paper towel.

"Hey, did I catch you at a bad time?" she asked as if she wanted me to say yes if it would free her from having to have this conversation.

I knew she was having issues with communicating with me. I can't blame her because I was a little pushy towards the end. Before she had changed her number, I even threatened to come to her office to make her talk to me although I knew I would never interrupt her work in that way. I would never have tried to embarrass her. Looking back, I could see how she might have thought I had gone off the deep end. I was crazy in love and was acting irrational.

"Nah, I'm good. I just got on the Beltway and I'm headed home," I offered. "what about you?"

I could hear the words from the Joe song I sent to her, and instantly I felt a sense of guilt. How could I have treated someone I proclaimed to love so much the way I did? She didn't deserve it. Although the fact that she was listening to the song was a good sign. There were three or four tracks on his latest CD that reminded me of what I'd gone through with her; the good and the bad. It was as if Joe was in my head and in my heart with this one.

What Keisha didn't know was that I was going to ask her to marry me after we'd been dating for a year. I had already picked out the ring and everything. It wasn't one of those tiny diamond rings either. This thing would send bat signals out to people all the way in Washington, DC from my home in Upper Marlboro.

"I'm not doing much of anything right now. I just got out of the shower," she said.

Visions of her in the shower crept into my mind. I reminisced back to us both in there washing each other's bodies and making love. That was normal for us.

"Keisha, I wanted to know if you would consider meeting me for dinner so that we can talk. I know I said I wouldn't put any pressure on you, but I would love to see you if only for an hour," I said not trying to sound like I was begging, although I was.

"You know what, Darius?" she said. "I think I'll take you up on that offer. Do you have any place in particular in mind?"

There was a moment of silence that lasted for what seemed like minutes. I wanted to make sure that I was hearing what I thought I was hearing before responding.

"Did you say you would meet me?" I asked surprisingly. I wasn't believing this.

"Yes, I did. Do you have time to meet me over at Bonefish Grill in Brandywine?" she asked.

"Of course, I'll meet you there. What time do you think you can make it?" I asked insisting that she make the next move. The ball was definitely in her court.

"Well, I've got a bunch of errands to run. How about this evening at 6:00?" She suggested.

"That sounds good to me. I'll see you there at 6:00," I said trying to contain my excitement. "Thanks, babe. You won't be sorry."

"I better not be," she joked. "I'll see you then."

I had a lot to do before 6:00. I needed to pick up my blue Armani suit from the cleaners and would definitely have to stop by a florist to get her some flowers. She loved pink roses, so I would have to find at least a dozen of those. She also loved purple, but looking for roses in any shade of purple on such short notice would be like looking for a needle in a hay stack. I'd have to make a mental note to remember to find some for the next time. It was already December, so the floral selections were limited for this time of year. Keisha was more into the flowers that bloomed in the spring and summer. Tulips were really her favorite, but you couldn't find those anywhere until the early part of spring.

After getting home, I took a long hot shower. The thought of her aroused me, as it always had. I tried to shake the thought of making love to her out of my mind by changing the water from hot to cold. After a couple of minutes of that, my body would behave for sure.

I dried myself off and sprayed on one of my favorite colognes that I knew she would remember. She always loved the way Gucci fragrances smelled on me. I ordered two dozen hot pink roses from the florist on Branch Avenue earlier that afternoon so they would be ready when I got there. I could easily get to Bonefish Grill from there. I just wanted things to be perfect for this dinner although Bonefish wasn't a place I would have selected. Don't get me wrong, the atmosphere was decent but I was thinking more along the lines of Fiola Mare in DC or someplace off the Potomac River. Something a little quieter and more romantic. But, it was her choice, so I went with it. The important thing is that we were going on a date, or at least having dinner together. I guess it depended on whose definition of a date you wanted to go with. To me, it was a date.

5 SO ANXIOUS

I scanned the Bonefish parking lot for Keisha's car, but from the looks of things, I wasn't going to be able to find it. I could barely find a parking space myself. With my racing heart and sweaty palms, I headed through the entrance to the restaurant. All eyes were on me as I headed toward the hostess stand. Wearing this suit was a smart decision. It generally yielded the kind of attention I was getting tonight. How Keisha felt was the only thing that mattered. I wanted her to see the man she loved and not just some guy who broke her heart because he couldn't live right.

"Good evening. Will you be dining with us alone?" asked the hostess. She was a beautiful young lady in her early twenties, probably a student from one of the area colleges. She looked like a Bowie State girl.

"No, I'm waiting for someone," I told her, scanning the restaurant to see if Keisha had already been seated.

"Hey, handsome," she said tapping my shoulder from

behind.

She looked absolutely gorgeous. This was nothing new; she always looked stunning. God had blessed her with the longest legs I'd ever seen on a woman. She was 5'9, but most of her height had to be taken up by those legs. Her beautiful brown eyes made it impossible for me to look at her for too long. I often found myself turning away so that I wouldn't be hypnotized by her. Once I looked deep within, I was gone. She was sporting a mid-length curly bob haircut and had dye it darker than her natural hair color since we had last seen each other. She was a show stopper wherever she went. A true stunner. For tonight, she was my superstar and everybody around us would know it. Handing her the hot pink roses I bought at the florist, I planted a kiss on her cheek. In my heart, I wanted to kiss her soft lips, but I decided not to; fearing what her response might be in front of the restaurant full of people. I didn't want to embarrass myself, but most importantly, I didn't want to push her away.

"Darius, why did you do that?" she asked with her dimpled smile. "You didn't have to bring me flowers."

"Baby Girl, you know I couldn't resist."

She knew I always brought flowers whenever we went on a date. If I picked her up at her place, I brought flowers. If we met someplace, I still brought flowers. That was just what I did. It was just a small gesture that indicated my feelings for her. She was a beautiful flower to me.

"What have I always told you? A woman as beautiful as you should always be showered with beautiful flowers and other pretty things. You look absolutely beautiful, you know that?" I asked trying to avoid her pretty brown eyes, but I failed. Once we locked eyes, I couldn't stop staring.

"I remember. Thanks, Darius," she said adjusting herself in her chair.

I sensed that she was a little uncomfortable, but I didn't

want to make things worse by asking. Just to have her here at the same table with me was more than enough right now. Maybe she would loosen up as the evening went on. At least I hoped she would. I had already planned on ordering a bottle of her favorite wine, or at least a glass to lighten her mood, although I would not be drinking any of it. She wasn't a big drinker, so one glass of wine and she would begin to loosen up. It didn't take much. Plus, she didn't know I had stopped drinking and I was hoping and praying that she would be happy to hear the news. Maybe she would even consider giving me another chance. An opportunity to fix the mess I made of our relationship. I didn't know how much time she would spend with me, but I was hoping we could continue this date even after dinner was over. I just wanted to talk to her. No pressure.

After the waitress took our orders, I stared at her from across the table for a moment. My heart ached for her and it was taking every bit of strength I had to keep from reaching across the table and taking her into my arms. I knew if I did, I would never let her go. Never again.

"You changed your hair," I said, reaching across the table to move strands that had fallen in her face and were now blocking one of her pretty brown eyes.

"Yes, I needed a change. Do you like it?" she smiled, striking a pose. "I see you shaved yours all off. I love it. You're very sexy with a bald head."

"Thanks. Keisha, yours looks absolutely beautiful! You know you could have shown up with a head full of rollers covered by a scarf and I would have thought you were the most beautiful woman in this place," I reminded her.

"You're still crazy," she said, tapping me on the arm from across the table. Her hand rested there.

"So, tell me why you finally agreed to have dinner with me?"

"Well, Darius, I figured it was time," she said, giving me a very serious look.

"Well, I am so happy that you did. I've been missing you like crazy, girl."

"I've been missing you too; although I was a little apprehensive about coming," she admitted, taking a sip of wine that had just been delivered to the table. "I just didn't want to get out here and have a repeat of the last time we went out. Remember Stacey's party?"

"Keisha, that's part of the reason why I wanted you to meet me for dinner. I wanted to tell you something," I said, pausing for a moment.

"Is Stacey all right?" she asked.

"Stacey's cool."

"Well, what's wrong? Is it DJ?" she asked in a panic.

"No, DJ's fine too. He's with his mother out in California right now. It's about me. I wanted to tell you that I stopped drinking," I said, looking into her eyes to see how she was feeling. "I joined AA several months ago and I've been going to counseling. Keisha, I haven't taken a drink in almost four months."

"Oh, my God," she said, reaching her hands toward me. "Baby, give me a hug!"

Four months was a major accomplishment for me considering I drank every single day after work and on the weekends prior to finding my sobriety.

"When you left me, I was devastated. I haven't been the same since. For weeks, I couldn't sleep. All I could think about was never being able to seeing you again. I didn't think I could make it without you. I need you so bad; I can't even put into words how bad."

"Well, Darius, I've been missing you too," she revealed, taking a sip from her wine glass. "Sweetie, I'm so sorry. Is this wine bothering you?"

"No, I can honestly say that I haven't even been tempted to take a drink. It doesn't bother me at all."

"Wow, are you serious? Is this the same Darius who could put away a twelve pack in a single bound?" she joked.

"Yes, it's me. What my alcoholism did to us was enough to scare me into stopping; I mean that." I admitted. "Being without you was the worst thing I've ever experienced."

"I am so proud of you that I don't even know what else to say. I wasn't expecting this. I am so glad I came here tonight," she admitted.

I couldn't believe she had finally admitted that she missed me. She was still the woman of my dreams; my soul-mate. This was going better than I expected. I asked God to bring her back, and now she was sitting across the table from me. I vowed I would never mess it up again if he brought her back. I also promised God I would never take another drink again. I had two promises to keep and I wasn't going to mess up either one of them. I put that on everything.

"Darius, I've thought about you so much since we broke up. When I changed my number, it was because I was just overwhelmed by everything that was going on. I don't want you to think that I'm making excuses," she held both of my hands in hers. "I know that love is supposed to be unconditional and I feel terrible about turning my back on you when you needed me. If I had it to do over again, it would have gone much differently. But you have to understand, the drinking was getting the best of me emotionally. It was wearing on me physically, and with my health problems, I just couldn't take care of someone who was as sick as you were with all the drinking. Physically, emotionally, and mentally; it destroyed us. I also wondered what would happen if I uprooted myself and made a new life down in Atlanta with the way things were. It wasn't a good idea, considering everything."

"Keisha, all I ever wanted to do was love you. Yes, I'm a recovering alcoholic. I know that now and I don't blame you for bailing out the way you did. I knew you needed to take care of yourself. I was on a path to self-destruction and I wasn't trying to hear that I was an alcoholic. I honestly didn't think that I was. It wasn't until you left me that I really came to understand what I am. I was standing on the balcony of my condo in Atlanta when I cried out to God with a beer in my hand. I was crying over the loss of our relationship as drunk as I could be. I asked God why? He spoke to me that night for the first time in my entire life. What he said to me changed my life forever. He told me if He couldn't trust me with my own life. How was He to trust me with yours?

"At that moment, the tears dried up. I went into the kitchen and poured out every alcoholic beverage that was in there and I haven't touched a drink since. I signed up for AA the very next day."

"That's deep. I am so thankful that God spoke to you about it. You don't know how happy that makes me," she said, sucking back the tears.

"Baby, if you'll just give me the chance to correct the mistakes I made with you I guarantee you won't be sorry. I've thought about no other woman but you since we broke up. I'd be lying if I said I didn't go on other dates, but no one could compare to you and none of those dates ever went anywhere. I was just going through the motions because that's what my boys told me I needed to do. I was trying to mask the pain."

"I know what you mean. I went through a brief relationship that didn't work out. I kept comparing him to you," she admitted. "He just didn't measure up, and never could. When you left for Atlanta, I wanted to go with you. I was willing to relocate just like we planned, but I was so afraid of getting down there away from everyone I loved; not to mention your illness. I was so afraid," she patted her eyes with a napkin to keep the tears from falling.

"Baby, it's all right. I understand now what you must have been going through. It was already enough to deal with right here at home with our friends and family all around us. It would have been very difficult to be down there with me drunk half the time and no one to turn to. It would have ended anyway."

"Besides, I did just up and leave in a hurry. It was barely thought out. We were chilling one day and the next thing I knew, I was out and setting up shop in the ATL."

"You were my world. Darius, you still are. I wish I could fix what happened, but all we can do now is try to move forward," she leaned back in her chair, staring at me for a response.

I knew at that moment I still had a chance and if so, I was never going to leave her. If I had to relocate again, Keisha would be coming with me as my wife. There was no doubt about that, or I wouldn't be going at all.

"So, are you saying you want to give it another try?" I asked, staring into her eyes for the truth. "You said you were single, right?"

"Yes, I'm single," she admitted, giving me half of a smile.

"Well, to be honest with you; I talked to Jamel. He told me you were single but I wanted to hear it from you. A brother doesn't want to get shot trying to take somebody else's lady because he didn't do good research."

She began to laugh. I had gotten her to finally loosen up like the Keisha I once knew. The wall that had been between us was finally coming down. We finished our dinner, not saying anything else about either of our past relationships. In fact, we enjoyed our meal with words unspoken; only stares that spoke volumes in our hearts. I had a lot of work to do if I was really going to get her back the way I wanted her. Just as I told her the day we met. She was going to share my last name one of these days. I spoke that back then and I would make it happen because I was a man of my word and she was the woman of my dreams.

We headed to my place after dinner to watch a movie just like we used to do when we were dating. It was nothing for us to spend a whole weekend doing absolutely nothing but cuddling up on the sofa watching movies. Keisha hadn't seen the Denzel Washington movie, Fences. I had just picked up the DVD the weekend before and couldn't think of anyone else I'd want to watch it with, but her. We popped some popcorn and snuggled on the sofa as if we'd never been apart. As long as she was sitting next to me, I was in Heaven. I prayed this was a long movie. I wanted to stay in this moment forever.

It was 1:00 AM when the movie ended and Keisha was fast asleep. I carried her to my room and placed her gently on the bed. After removing her shoes, I placed a blanket over her and kissed her on the cheek. Watching her sleep made my heart ache. I was so in love with this woman that I wanted to climb behind her in bed and hold her close. Instead, I opted to watch her sleep from the doorway to my room if only for a few minutes.

I slept in one of the guestrooms that night, although I wanted to take what I believed was my rightful place in my bed next to her. Out of respect, I thought it best to separate myself from her; to maintain my self-control. There would be plenty of time to make love to her later. Right now, it was about fixing the mess I'd made of our relationship, regaining her trust, and getting her to see how important her love was to me. Having her here in my home was more important than a couple of hours of hot, steamy love-making could ever be. I wanted more than that. I wanted forever with her.

6 LIKE OLD TIMES

I got out of bed at 8:00 so I could be ready before Darius arrived. The weather was going to hit 70 degrees today, which was unusual for Maryland this late in the year. He had volunteered to wash my car and to cut the grass for what I hoped was the last time until spring. I was never big on yard work, and would willingly pay a landscaping company to come out here to handle it; but Darius volunteered to take care of it. I jumped into the shower and put on a sexy pair of jeans with a new top I'd bought at Nordstrom's last week. I was trying to get his attention without making it so obvious. Because we would be out in the yard, I figured jeans would be much more attractive than sweats. Besides, I knew he wasn't going to let me get dirty anyway. That's just how he was.

I decided there was still enough time to make breakfast before he showed up. He loved turkey sausage, pancakes and scrambled eggs with cheese. He always mixed orange and apple juice together to drink with his meal. Even when we went out for breakfast, he always ordered both and then mixed them. The thought made me smile. Pouring the combination of juices into a large glass, I couldn't help but wonder how we got here? Just as I was about to put the glasses on the table, the doorbell rang.

"Hey there," I said, kissing his cheek.

"Good morning, beautiful," he said. "Did you get anymore rest after you drove home this morning?" he asked.

"Yes, a couple of hours, although I slept better at your place. In fact, I'm so well rested that I decided to get up early this morning to make you breakfast," I teased.

"I thought I smelled some turkey sausage!" Surprised by the spread that had been prepared just for him. He headed straight for the kitchen to wash his hands before taking his place at the table. A spot no one else had occupied since we broke up.

We enjoyed a nice, quiet breakfast together before heading out into the yard. I was having a great time with him and was already thinking of a reason for him to stay after we'd finished the chores for the day.

"Baby, could you bring me another sponge?" he asked. "These rims look terrible! I can't have you rolling around in a 750 looking like this! I can tell nobody's been taking care of this since I left."

I smiled, handing him a sponge, and the tire and rim cleaner. He was really putting some muscle into it just like he used to do when he washed my car every single week. He was a good man, and I was happy to have him back in my life. I was so in love with him; so much I couldn't even put it into words. I was so glad I had been able to finally admit some things. Glad that we both had the chance to confess. He vowed not to ever leave me again. I wasn't going anywhere either. This was it for me. The last hoorah.

"What are you doing later?" Turning the extra bucket

upside down, I took a seat next to where he was working.

"I hadn't really thought about it. You have something in mind?" he asked, looking at me for a response.

"Well, I was going to cook something tonight. You want to stay for dinner? I mean, you've been working your butt off out here. The least I can do is feed you," I joked, splashing water from the bucket at him.

"Do you think I'd be crazy enough to say no? I've been trying to spend some time with my favorite girl for how many months now?" he teased. "That sounds like a good idea to me."

"Okay, it's settled. If you want to, we can watch a movie or something. I was going to bake a lasagna, make a salad and some Italian bread. How does that sound?"

"Sounds like a date to me. After I finish this, I'm going home to shower and change and then I'll come back," he said. "Do you need me to pick up anything?"

"No, I've got everything I need," I said. I meant that literally.

He finished washing the car and then cut the grass while I pulled weeds out of the flowerbed in front of the house. While he was edging the walkway, I looked over and gave him a big smile. A month ago, I probably would have ignored an e-mail just to keep from opening old wounds. I didn't even know why I'd opened the last one. Well, I do know. God was guiding me in that decision. At least, I wanted to believe He was. It was because of Him that we ended up here right now. God's hand was all in it. We had come back full circle.

I knew that I would eventually have to face Candice, his mother. We hadn't spoken since Darius and I parted ways. I know she thought it was my fault because everyone who knew us could see what the break up was doing to him. I didn't know what he might have said to her, but I would need to clear the air between us because I needed us to be okay if

Darius and I were going to work out our problems. I couldn't stand not having her in my life because of bitterness or animosity. I would have to apologize for my part in the break up. I would have to take care of that real soon. She was the mother-in-law I always wanted and I had ruined any chance of that when we broke up. I needed to salvage any part of our relationship. She thought I'd not only bailed out on Darius, but had abandoned DJ too. That hurt me deeply, because I knew it was the truth.

DJ remained in town for a month after his father headed to Atlanta and I didn't call him one time after we broke up. I was so mad at Darius that I made DJ suffer along with him. I was so wrong for that and couldn't blame Candice if she never forgave me for it. I would at least have to try. I knew I owed her that much. I also owed it to DJ and would have to ask forgiveness from him too. He was my boy. We had a great relationship and could do things together, just the two of us. I wanted to get that back, but only after I apologized for leaving him at a time when he really needed me to be there. He was a great kid and didn't deserve how I'd treated him.

After removing the weeds, I went into the house to take the ground turkey out of the freezer. I grabbed two ice cold bottles of water before heading back outside. By now, Darius had removed his shirt. There it was. The tattoo he'd gotten to celebrate our six-month anniversary. My name in bold letters written across his chest. I often wondered how he would explain that to anyone he became intimate with after we broke up. I might ask him someday, or maybe I wouldn't. It didn't matter anymore anyway, because no one else would have to look at it ever again but me.

"Here, babe," handing him one of the bottles of water.
He drank it in ten seconds flat.
"Man, you were thirsty! Do you want this one?" I asked.

"No, I'm good. Thanks, though. I'm about to head to the house to get cleaned up. I should be back in less than an hour," he said.

It would be a couple of hours before I started cooking dinner, so we would be spending the rest of the day together, just like old times. I was so excited I could feel the butterflies roaming around my stomach. Although we'd been here plenty of times before, it felt different now. I suppose it was because we both knew what we wanted and were going to make this relationship the best that it could be. No drama and no drinking.

7 ADDICTED

"Keisha, you really put everything you had into this dinner," I told her, shoving another forkful of lasagna in my mouth. "It's absolutely delicious, babe. I've missed your good cooking."

"It's okay," she said modestly, exposing the dimples I loved so much. They were so deep, I loved sticking my finger in them.

"Well you did a great job at it, no matter what you did," I told her. "You know you put your foot in it!"

After we finished dinner, she brought dessert into the family room so we could eat while watching a movie. My baby knew I loved cheesecake, so she baked one especially for me that was topped with my favorite; glazed strawberries. After watching the second movie, I started getting a little tired, but I was not about to leave. I was enjoying the evening and would stay up all night as long as I could be in her company. I feared falling asleep, and waking up only to realize it was all a dream. The thought of that being the case was more like a nightmare to me. I didn't want to face the reality that this might not move past the early stages of a relationship because we'd been here before. I knew what she was capable of. She'd left me once and she could do it again. So, if it meant staying awake all night, I would do that just to stay in the moment for however long it lasted.

Her head rested on my shoulder while she slept and I didn't want to disturb her by trying to get into a more comfortable position; so, I laid my head back and drifted off to sleep just the same. I woke up two hours later with her still fast asleep in the same position. She looked like an angel.

"Keisha, wake up, baby." The selfish part of me wanted to leave her asleep in my arms on the sofa. The warmth of her body next to mine was bringing back so many memories. Times that held a special place within me forever.

"Huh? What's wrong?" She looked around the room, trying to get her bearings. "You were asleep. Why don't you go ahead to bed," I insisted. "It's getting late, and I should probably go so you can get some rest."

"I don't want you to leave. Why don't you come and lay down with me?" Reaching for my hand, she led me to her bedroom.

The room looked much different than how I remembered it. The furniture was rearranged to make the room look more spacious. The walls were painted in a shade that resembled eggnog. She had changed the curtains and comforter set, and added a couple of very large potted plants. It looked like something out of *Better Homes and Gardens*. The smell of ginger and peaches filled the room. There were two candles burning on the dresser and several in the bathroom; which had also been expanded to three times its' original size since I'd last been here.

Keisha began to unbutton her shirt as she stared into my eyes. Not saying a word, I helped her with the last two buttons. She let it fall to the floor before stepping out of her jeans. She looked so beautiful to me as she stood there wearing nothing but a hot pink bra and panty set that could only have come from Victoria's Secret, one of her favorite places. The shade of pink against her smooth, caramel colored skin made my heart flutter. I wanted her so badly, I could taste it.

"Come here," I pulled her so close to me I could feel the heat from her body. "I've missed holding you like this."

She took one step back and unbuttoned my shirt. I removed one arm and then the other before tossing it on the floor. She unbuckled my belt, freeing my body from my jeans. My breathing became heavy and I wanted to take her into my arms again; but I waited for her to make the next move. Keisha reached for the waistband of my boxers, and pulled them down, forcing me to step out of them. My body responded in a way that made me embarrassed. Keisha had seen it so many times before, but this time was different. The woman of my dreams; the one I thought I'd have to learn to live without was standing less than an arms' reach in front of me wearing almost nothing. We were about to go someplace that would bond us together; this time for an eternity. I would make sure this time around would be better than anything she could ever imagine. I was certain I was never letting her go again. In relationships gone bad, rarely do you ever get a second chance to right the wrongs that were done. I was getting another opportunity, and I would cherish it for as long as I had air to breathe.

Reaching out, I pulled her closer so I could kiss her soft, beautiful lips. I needed to feel them so badly. In a moment of passion, we were intertwined in a caress that sent my heart into a rapid beat. Freeing her beautiful breasts from her bra, I dropped it to the floor. Her panties soon followed.

I kissed her on the side of her neck, and backed her up

to the bed before laying her down. I knew that our lives would never be the same from this moment on. She grabbed me in a way that she'd never done before, but it felt so familiar. We were trying to slowly get reacquainted with each other. In my heart, I knew that we should probably wait; but I wasn't thinking with my heart at that moment. I was thinking with my mind. They say the brain is stupid, and to listen to your heart. Right now, I knew what I wanted so the difference between doing what's right and doing what's wrong went out the window.

"Oh," she whispered. "I've been missing you so much."

"I've missed you too, babe."

I grabbed a breast in each of my hands and stared at them.

"This is so wrong, but I can't resist," I admitted.

"Oh, Darius," Keisha caressed the back of my head with both hands.

I wanted to indulge in her just like old times. This time, I wouldn't take any of it for granted. Before, we made love so much I just expected it every day. Now, I was ready to cherish this woman; my woman. Pleasing her was my priority, but I wanted to go about it in the right way. I wanted to drive her crazy with my love from the inside out; better than I'd ever pleased her before. But I also wanted to make her my wife before we went any further.

I was so high when I made love to her that the temptation was so hard to ignore. She was like a drug that I couldn't free myself of. Better than any intoxicating drink I'd ever had. She was my addiction and there was no cure for this. Seeing Keisha through sober eyes was so amazing, I wanted to cry. She was the only one I had ever shed tears for; I was fighting back a bunch of them right now.

"Do you have condoms?" She asked.

"Yes, but we have all night, and I want to enjoy every

moment of this."

Keisha was in the driver's seat. She knew what she wanted to do. I fumbled for the pack of Magnums that were in the pocket of my jeans. Ripping the perforation to separate one from the other, I placed the others on the nightstand next to the bed.

"I just want to love you nice and slow."

I missed this woman so much that I feared not being able to perform. I wanted so badly to please her. Keisha used to tell me that I was the best she'd ever had, and that I knew how to please her. I wanted to make sure I still measured up. I knew she had slept with someone after we broke up. Maybe he was better and more skilled than me. But, then again, if he was she might still be with him. I had to put that thought out of my mind if I was going to do this right.

"Darius, I can't stand it anymore." She moaned.

I ignored her for a few seconds more.

"Oh, baby," she said, "please don't stop."

I rolled the condom on and the room faded to black. What seemed like five minutes had turned out to be two hours. Back in the day, we used to engage in continuous foreplay. It lasted from sun up to sun down. I knew how to get her in the mood and how to keep her there.

"Oh, Darius," she moaned. "Was that good to you?"

"Yes, baby. It was just like I remembered it. All I've thought about since I laid eyes on you the other day is being with you. Making love to you." I admitted while holding her tightly in my arms. I didn't want to let her go.

I wanted to feel the deepest part of her and wasn't about to rush it. I wanted to savor every moment of the love we shared, although guilt consumed me. Keisha had always been the one more spiritually grounded. She was the one who went to church every Sunday and Bible study once a week before she got caught up with me. I had been a bad influence and I felt terrible about it.

"I'm going to make an honest woman out of you. I promised I would and my word is more important to me than a lot of things."

"We can talk about that later."

"I've never been with any woman who I thought was wifey material. No woman who could please me the way that I need to be pleased, love me the way that I need to be loved. No other who understands me. You know how to calm me when I'm troubled. No one else can do any of that, but you."

"That's the connection that we have, Darius. I suppose that's why we've ended up back here."

"You're right," I planted a kiss on her forehead as she rested on my shoulder.

Kissing her again on her cheek, I tasted her salty tears. They were flowing down her face uncontrollably.

"What's wrong, babe?" I asked, wiping them away.

"Nothing's wrong, baby," she said, "I just missed you so much. I'm just so overjoyed, it hurts."

"I know what you mean. I love you more than you could ever know." I held her tightly in my arms. I knew we were finally on track; headed toward forever and never looking back. I would be there for her and would love her until the end of our time.

In my heart, I knew I would be headed to the jewelry store before the end of the week. My love was back, and I was gonna put the biggest rock on her finger that my money could buy. I would probably have to get help from Jamel or one of her girlfriends because I wanted the ring to be right, the proposal, the whole nine yards. Lying in bed with my hands folded under my head, I plotted out my next move while my baby rested silently next to me fast asleep.

8 DON'T WAKE ME IF I'M DREAMING

I woke up to the smell of candles burning at 4:00 AM. Darius was fast asleep in the spot he had occupied so many nights before. When we dated the first time, it was not uncommon for him to be at my place or for me to be at his. In fact, the entire relationship that's the way things went. From the first night we slept together, we didn't spend another night alone. He was resting so peacefully that all I could do was watch him rest. Last night was such an incredible night, we even made love in my dreams. My fear was waking up and discovering that I really had dreamed the whole ordeal, so I couldn't help but smile when I found him lying in the same place I'd left him. I walked over to the dresser, blew out the candles and climbed back into bed, snuggling close to him.

I could feel the hardness of him resting against my back, so I knew he was ready for another round. I guess some things never changed; I was so glad it hadn't. To me, the best sex came during the early hours of the morning before the sun came up. All we had to do was make love. No words needed. Our bodies spoke a special language.

Darius's sex game was even better sober than it was when he was intoxicated. Back then, we used to do some crazy things. He had turned me into the type of person who would try anything once. I had never been like that before, but if I enjoyed it, we incorporated it into our regular love making. If I didn't, we just didn't do it again. Now, don't get me wrong. I wasn't into threesomes or anything like that. I didn't believe in sharing my man with anyone. I still don't believe in that. Our likes and dislikes were so similar that it was amazing. There weren't too many positions we hadn't tried. The truth is, he was so good that I'd make love to him while hanging upside down from a treehouse swing if he asked me to. Some of the things we'd done, I was too embarrassed to admit to and would never share any of the stories with my girlfriends out of fear that I would be judged.

"Roll over on your stomach," he whispered, guiding my body into the appropriate position.

Not saying a word, I rolled over. He kissed the nape of my neck; remembering the sensitive spot he knew would send a tingling sensation running through my entire body. Whatever Darius wanted me to do, I would do it. He knew everything I liked; and from the moment our bodies touched last night, it was all so familiar as if we'd never missed a day together.

After kissing every inch of the back of my body, he rolled me over. He started kissing my neck and then my stomach, making it difficult for me to maintain control. He rested his head there for a moment.

"I want you to be my wife. I want you to have my babies."

"Turn over," he said.

"Whatever you want, baby."

Darius held my body close to him as he delivered

another dose of his love. We laid in each other's arms daydreaming in a place we'd tried to visit before, but got lost. It was forever and we were on that road again. This time, we took a one-way street, and there were no U-turns allowed. This time, there was something different, but I didn't know what it was.

I often thought of how much of a fool I was for letting him get away before. Don't get me wrong because sex isn't everything. It wasn't about that. The way he made me feel was incredible, so I knew it was an important part but not the largest part of what we shared. I just loved this man and would do everything I could to keep him in my life this time. We were not going to lose what we had. I would support him in any way I could to help him stay on the right track in his sobriety. Darius taught me what unconditional love was. He always loved me unconditionally, but I didn't love him that way in return. I was sorry for that.

"You okay, baby girl?" he asked, rubbing my hair in soft slow strokes.

"I couldn't be any better than I am right now; and you?" I asked, bringing my head to rest on his shoulder.

"I'm with you. I'm where I'm supposed to be, so I have no complaints."

"I'm just so sorry we lost so much time."

"Keisha, I've been lost without you. Since the day we broke up, I haven't been the same. From this moment on, I'm living in the here and now. That's what matters to me."

"I know what you mean. I tried to move on, but it just didn't work because I was still in love with you. After things ended; I was devastated, and there wasn't a single day I didn't think of you. I even thought about showing up in Atlanta to try to win you back, but I was afraid of what I might have found when I got there, so I chickened out," I confessed. "I didn't want to get my feelings hurt if I ran up on you and another woman. Someone you loved more than me. I wasn't sure how I would react, so the best thing for me to do at the time was to stay right here in Maryland."

"Can you promise me one thing?" he asked.

"Yes, what is it?" I inquired, waiting for him to say what was on his mind.

"Can you absolutely promise me you'll never leave me again, no matter what?"

"Darius, I put my life on it. I've never had anyone give me the honesty and love that you've given me. I can absolutely promise you, I'll never leave you again. I want to share my entire world with you. You're my one and only true love. They say love is better the second time around if you're lucky enough to get the opportunity. You learn so much the first time that the second time can only be better, right?"

"You're right. Trust me. If I knew some of the things back then that I know now, we would have never broken up. I put a lot on you back then and I would never do that again. I didn't realize it but, I was not only killing myself; but I was killing you too. Not literally, but emotionally. So, we just vowed to never part again. That means the world to me."

We sealed our commitment with a kiss and went back to sleep. I could have stayed in bed all day as long as I was in the comfort of his strong arms. There was absolutely nothing that could get in the way of what we had; the love we shared. I was in total bliss when I was with him and wouldn't trade the feeling for anything in the world. The trust we shared with each other was like nothing I'd ever experienced before. I never once thought that he would cheat on me. Even when he was drinking, it was the farthest thing from my mind. Now that he was sober, it was even less of a concern for me. Darius loved me, and this I was certain of. We didn't have those types of problems like other people did in their relationships. I wanted to wake up next to him every morning. Out of all the relationships I'd ever been in, I never saw myself headed toward forever before. I never wanted to experience sex, love, or even a kiss with anyone else but him.

"Keish?"

"Yes, baby."

"Remember when I told you that you would one day share my last name? That day in the Food Lion parking lot when we first met, you thought I was talking crazy. I meant what I said."

"I know you did, babe. I know." Smiling, I turned my back to him and snuggled tightly against his body.

I knew that the day would eventually come when he would ask me to marry him. I also knew what my answer would be. I couldn't wait to be Mrs. Darius Kingston. I would wear his last name like a badge of honor that no one could take away from me.

Suddenly, I realized what was different about the last round of lovemaking. This time, there was no condom. The remaining two magnums were still on the nightstand. I wasn't sure how I felt about it. I mean, I was in love with him and knew that I was going to spend the rest of my life with him. I'd had protected sex three times with someone else. He'd had sex with one other person, prayerfully with protection. What's done was done. I would have to ask him about it later just for peace of mind. I guess it was too late to dwell on that now. We'd already done it.

9 KEISHA & JAMEL

Performance appraisals were my top priority today. I had written two so far with eight more to go. I was realizing that hiring half a team of new employees on the same day had its' disadvantages. Their evaluations would all be due at the same time. So, I was in my office with the door closed for most of the day, pounding away at the keys so each one of them would get what they truly deserved. One thing they could all say about me is that I was fair, and always gave credit, recognition and praise where it was due.

"Keisha, you have a call on line two. Keisha, line two," said Angela, one of the branch representatives over the loud speaker.

"This is Keisha, may I help you?"

"Hey babe, what in the heck is this I'm hearing about you and my boy?"

"Hi, Jamel. How are you?"

"Don't act like you didn't hear me. What's up? Monica told me she saw you and D. at Bonefish Grill the other night. Did you actually think for one second that you were going out like that and I wouldn't find out? You know I've got people all around PG County and they tell me everything. There's not much you can get by me, Keisha. Besides, I thought I was your boy! I mean, when Darius reached out to me to see how you were doing and to ask if you were single, I didn't know he was making a move that soon. I mean, really?"

"I was going to call you, but I've been so busy. Well, if Monica saw us, why didn't she come over to say hello? She probably couldn't wait to tell it."

"Nah, she was over there with Rico. I guess she was doing her own thing and didn't want to interfere. You remember Rico, right? Apparently, they've been spending a lot of time together lately. I'm not sure what she sees in him, but that's her business."

"Yeah, isn't he that dancer from The Class Act? So, she's hanging out with him now, huh? I'm really surprised because he doesn't strike me as her type at all. I thought they were just friends, not friends with benefits."

"Yeah, she said they're just friends but again, it's none of my business," said Jamel, trying not to let his agitation show through his tone. He knew Rico was a loser, but still remained cordial to him whenever Monica brought him around out of respect for her. "Anyway, I didn't call you to talk about Monica and Rico. What in the world is up with you, baby? Tell me about your date! How did you two hook back up?"

"Well, Darius contacted me a couple of days ago; and I don't know what came over me. You know I've been avoiding him like the plague. He sent an e-mail and I was simply going to shoot him a quick reply, but decided to call instead. Meanwhile, he asked me to meet up with him but I told him I needed time to think about it. After the call ended, I clicked on a link in the email and it was a love song by Joe. Have you heard the one, "If You Lose Her?" Darius was always sending me songs that reminded him of us."

"Yes, I've heard it. Not to mention, aren't you one of Joe's biggest fans? How many times have you seen that man in concert? At least ten, right? Keisha, I know you better than that. I was there when you and Darius dated before, remember? You know you still love him. I don't know why you're acting like you don't. Truth be told, I thought you were gonna ride or die until the end with him. I was shocked when you decided to get rid of him."

"Yeah, I know. It was pretty deep, wasn't it? But still, I was trying to resist the temptation until I listened to that song. I don't know what it is, but it's almost like Joe's been living in our relationship. So many of his songs remind me of what we went through. So, I made the decision that night to agree to go out to dinner with him when we spoke the next day."

"Well, you know what? Dinner never hurt anyone and besides, you'll know whether his heart is sincere as time progresses. I just hate to see you get caught up with him if he's still drinking. That was difficult to watch. How many times did you end up in Sickle Cell Crisis because you were worried about him?"

"There were a couple of episodes, but I think it was a culmination of events that always landed me in the hospital. I would never stand for that again. Oh, and I forgot to tell you! He's not drinking anymore!"

"What the??? So, you made the man sober up, huh? Well, the two of you were inseparable. You were at your happiest when you were with him, but also at your worst because of all the drinking. I just want you to be happy and if Darius makes you happy, then I'm all for it. I must admit I am a little bit jealous because I couldn't seem to get even a few hours with you. Up until Darius came into the picture, you used to have mad love for me; but after he showed up it was like, Jamel? Who's that?"

"You're so silly."

"All jokes aside. Are you two together, or what? I mean,

if you are I'm all for it. You know you're my baby and Darius is my boy. If anybody is gonna snatch up a beautiful queen like you, then I'm glad it's him."

"Yeah, well. We did decide we were gonna give it another try. In fact, I really believe this is it, Jamel. You and I can talk about anything, right?"

"Haven't we always been able to?"

"Ok, here it is. We spent the entire weekend together. We made love just like old times. It was just like I remembered it. His body . . ."

"Keisha, I don't need a visual. Spare me the details. I get your point. Hum, I've been kicked to the curb again. I guess the closest I'll get to hearing your voice from here on out will be listening to your voice mail."

Jamel knew that he was happy that Darius and I were back together. He took the breakup harder than anyone. Jamel and Darius were cool and used to hang out together when he wasn't with me. Darius would invite him and some of the other guys over to watch sports. They even went to happy hour several times in the past. Yes, we were together a lot, but it was also nothing for the three of us to grab a bite to eat or check out a movie. Darius never had a concern for the relationship I shared with Jamel. We always had a mutual trust in that way.

"You know you're still my Boo," I reminded him. "I've got to get ready to go for now, though. I'm writing reviews and I really need to get back to work."

"Okay, just give me a call when you guys come up for air," he joked.

"Bye, Jamel. Love you!"

"I love you to, beautiful."

Placing his cell phone back on his hip, Jamel shook his head. Yes, he was happy that Keisha and Darius were back together; but in the back of his mind he wondered if Darius had truly given up drinking. He didn't want Keisha to get her heart broken. He couldn't stand to watch her go through what she went through the first time. He made a mental note to talk to Darius to see where his head was. He would just have to keep it real with him by letting him know that he wasn't tolerating any of what he put her through the first time. Jamel was very protective of her and had been since college. They had been friends way too long to not have her back when it came to matters of the heart. She was like a sister to him and he would protect her no matter what.

Jamel was right about one thing. Darius and I were known for spending all our private time together. DJ spent a lot of time with his mother, who was cool with me. She never tried to cause any problems for us while we were dating. We were always cordial to one another, which was kind of unusual because baby's mamas don't always act right. Denise was different. She minded her own business and never showed any signs of jealousy. She never said anything bad about Darius and had even told me once that he was a good man. He just wasn't the one for her. I respected what she had to say, and was so thankful she wasn't a drama queen. In all honesty, if half the men with an ex or baby's mama out there had one like Denise, life would be grand for them all.

I made it through four more appraisals before the end of the workday. I was going to take the rest home, but opted not to because Darius was bringing dinner over. We were starting again with the daily visits. I didn't have a problem with it, but did tell him that each of us deserved some "me" time every now and then. He agreed. We were trying to take a different approach this time and didn't want to get overwhelmed by always being in each other's faces.

The chime of the door alarm alerted me to Darius's presence. He still had his key from the last time, and I had told him it was okay to start using it again. I took one of the bags from him and placed it on the island so I could welcome him home with a big hug and kiss.

"How's my baby doing today?" He asked.

He softly kissed my lips. Smacking me on the butt, he went to the refrigerator to grab a bottle of water. "Before I forget; Jamel wants you to give him a call when you get a chance. I talked to him earlier. That man's a fool, isn't he?"

"I know. He called me at work today to grill me about what's going on with us. Apparently, Monica saw us when we were having dinner the other night."

"Yeah, he told me. So, what did you tell him?"

"The truth, the whole truth and nothing but the truth," I joked. "He didn't want the details. Besides, don't act like the two of you didn't talk about it too."

"Yeah, I told him I was tappin' it again and that you've been missing big daddy since I left."

"You better stop playin'. I know you didn't tell him that!"

"Okay, no I didn't say all that. He wants us to hang out Saturday night. He said something about having a get together at his place. He invited a couple of his people from work and he wants us to join him. He said he invited Monica and Rico and a couple of his cousins too. You know, the regular crew."

"Oh; sounds like he's got it all planned out."

"What about your girls, Pam and Shawn? He said he wanted you to invite them."

"I haven't spoken to them in a minute, but I suppose this would be a good time to call them. I haven't even told them we're back together yet."

"What you waiting for? I thought they would have been the first ones you called. I thought you told them everything."

"Shawn's out of town and won't be back until

tomorrow. Pam, as judgmental as she is; needs to be told in bits and pieces. Oh, and my mother was the first person I told. Jamel was the second. The ladies don't know a thing yet."

"You afraid of what they might say?"

"I really don't care what either of them has to say. It's not going to change anything. I just haven't had time, but I'll get to it."

"Well, call them and invite them over to Jamel's. He said Saturday night at 7:00."

"Okay. It would be fun to have the gang all together. We haven't gotten together like this in several months. Life just took everybody in different directions; and although we talked over the phone, we emailed or sent text messages more than anything else. Pam, Shawn and I met for dinner once a month. Sometimes Monica would join us, but that was about it. So, yes. I better call them."

Monica was actually my closest friend, but since she'd started dating Rico the Freak-o, as Shawn often called him; I didn't get to see her that often. Getting everyone in the same place at the same time was a rare occasion.

I went into the bedroom while Darius unpacked the take-out he'd picked up from Cheddar's. I dialed Shawn's number first. She would be the easiest one to tell.

"Hey, girl," it's me.

"What you been up to," Shawn asked.

"This and that."

"Girl, me too. I'll be so glad to get back home tomorrow, it's not even funny. I'm so tired of living out of a suitcase. This job is about to work my nerves with all this travel. I mean, I've been on the go so much, I feel like I've taken up residency at the Hilton."

"You scheduled to go on anymore long distance trips before the holidays?"

"No, this is it. I can't take much more; I need a break! My poor kids are starting to forget they have a mother."

"They're all right. I talked to Tyrone a couple of days ago to make sure they were okay."

"Thank God for him. He's the greatest ex-husband and father that a woman could ever have prayed for. Sometimes I forget we're divorced."

"You know you still got him wrapped around your little finger. I don't know why you acting like you don't still love him."

"I never said I didn't. That chick showing up on my doorstep with a baby that looked just like him was enough to make me let it go, though. The only reason why he does the things he does for me is because he knows he messed up and this is his way of letting me know how sorry he is. I know he still loves me, but his cheating was too much. I mean, I put up with a lot. I took what I could, but a baby? No, that was too much for me. I forgive him, but that one is beyond my level of forgetting what happened. I see myself throwing it in his face every time I would have to look at that baby. He made his bed; now he has to deal with the consequences."

"It is what it is, I guess. Oh, I almost forgot why I was calling. Jamel is having a get together Saturday night at around 6:30. He wants you to be there."

Shawn was late for everything. You always had to tell her a little white lie by pushing the time back by at least thirty minutes. If you told her 6:30, she might be there by 7:00.

"That sounds like a plan. I'll be there because I haven't seen Jamel in a minute. Everybody's been so busy doing their own thing. Who's supposed to be there?"

"You know; the usual crew. I know Pam, you, me, Stacey, Steve, Monica and her man, Rico; some guys from work and Darius. Oh, and couple of Jamel's cousins who are in town for a visit will be there. I'm about to call Pam in a minute to tell her too."

"Okay, well tell her I said hello. I'll see you guys on Saturday."

"Have a safe trip."

I hung up the phone quickly so I wouldn't have to spend the next hour explaining what I've been up to. I immediately dialed Pam's number.

"Hey, Pam. What's up?"

"Hey, Keisha. I just got finished putting the dishes in the dishwasher. What's going on?"

The other line beeped before I could answer. Shawn's mind must have just registered what I'd said. She was calling back for confirmation.

"Pam, hold on a second. Let me get Shawn off the other line."

"Hello?"

"What the what? Did you say Darius was gonna be there?"

"Yes, Darius is back and we're actually seeing each other again."

"Well dang! I leave town for a few days and you two end up back together? I ain't mad at cha. What's been going' on with him? Is he still living in Atlanta? What about all that drinking?"

"Girl, that's the thing. He's not drinking anymore. He's been attending AA meetings and going to counseling and everything, and he's back in PG County. It's a long story. I'll tell you about it later, but Pam's on the other line."

"Okay. You better call me back. I'm not playing with you."

"Bye, Shawn."

"Peace."

I clicked back over to Pam.

"Pam, I'm sorry. That was Shawn. She told me to tell

you hello."

"She back in town yet?"

"She'll be back tomorrow."

"Before I forget. Jamel wanted me to call you because he's having a get together on Saturday night. He said to come over around 7:00."

Pam was always prompt, so she didn't need a thirty-minute buffer like Shawn did.

"Does he need me to bring anything?"

"He didn't say, but I was going to make some meatballs and maybe some wings or something."

"You handle the meatballs, I'll take care of the wings," Pam said. "I'll call him to see if he needs anything else."

"Sounds like a plan."

"Cool. I'll talk to you later."

"Oh, before you go. I have to tell you something."

"What is it, girl?"

"Guess who I'm seeing now?"

"Let me guess. Darius!"

"How'd you know?"

"A blind man could have seen that coming. You two should have never broken up in the first place. I mean, he was drinking a lot and all; but I believed you could have saved him, though. You just needed to bring him to church more."

"Well, that's another thing. He's not drinking anymore. He said he's been sober for four months."

"Praise God!"

"You can say that again."

"Girl, on that note, I'm hanging up."

"See you Saturday. We'll probably talk before then."

I hung up the phone and went back to Darius. We were having our dinner by candlelight. He had picked up crab cakes, shrimp Alfredo and salad from Cheddar's. He knew I was a fan of anything with seafood in it. Dinner was delicious, but I just wanted to be in his arms. I had already gotten used to it being the norm.

10 SURPRISE!

Pam and I met at Jamel's house at about 6:15. Meatballs, pasta salad, and fruit and vegetable trays were my contribution to the party. With Pam's chicken wings and spinach dip and Shawn's mini ham sandwiches, deviled eggs and banana pudding; I'd say we had a pretty good spread. My baby ordered mini crab cakes and shrimp cocktail from Phillip's Seafood that was supposed to be delivered by 6:30, so Pam and I figured we could get everything else all set up and ready to go prior to the delivery. In the year and a half that Jamel had been living in the new house, we'd broken his kitchen in pretty good.

"Keisha, what time is Shawn coming?" Pam asked.

"You know how she does. I told her 6:30, so we'll hopefully see her by 7:00."

"You told her 6:30?"

"Don't you always back the time up on her?"

"Yeah, you got a point. That girl is late for church every Sunday."

"She's late for everything. You've got to love her!"

We put the tablecloths on the tables Jamel had bought for the party.

"What in the world is up with all of this lavender and

purple stuff? Is Jamel changing up on us or what?"

"Girl, you're stupid! I don't know, I guess he's developed a fondness for purple; although this looks more like periwinkle to me."

"Whatever, Pam rolled her eyes."

I looked out the family room window to see who was ringing the doorbell. Shawn's car was there. So was the Phillip's delivery truck.

"Come on in," I told the driver. "Hey, Shawn. I can't believe you're actually on time."

I directed him to place the trays on the table and handed him a $40 tip before walking him back to the door.

"How much food did Darius order?" Pam asked.

"Girl, you know how he is. Remember my last birthday party? He ordered so much food; we were brown bagging it to work for a week. I ended up taking some of it to work and the girls ate it for two days. Now you know if you have enough food left over for twenty people to eat for two days without running out of anything; there was way too much."

"Where's Jamel?" Shawn asked.

"I don't know where he is. I had to use my key to get in. He did call my cell phone right before I got here to say he'd be here in a little while, though."

"Oh, okay."

We were organizing things in the dining room when Darius showed up. He walked in looking as fine as ever in a tailor made black suit accented with a lavender shirt and coordinating tie. He was looking so good, I couldn't wait to get him home so I could get him out of that suit.

"Baby, you sure are looking good! You're definitely working that lavender shirt!"

"Thanks, love. Hi Pam, Shawn," he turned his attention to them for a second; giving each of them a kiss on the cheek.

"What's up, Darius? It's been a long time. You really are

looking good. I'm really feeling the bald head," Shawn admitted. "You better take care of my girl," she whispered in his ear.

"I got this," he smiled, glancing in my direction.

"Baby, call Jamel to see where he is. This is his party and we're here doing all the work. How fair is that?"

"He's outside. I saw him when I pulled up. Monica and Rico are out there too."

"Oh, okay."

Jamel came into the house carrying bags full of ice, cases of beer, wine, sparkling cider, and sodas. Monica and Rico followed carrying grocery bags full of chips, crackers, dips and salsa, and a huge cake.

"Babe, are you going to be all right with the beer and wine everywhere?"

"Sweetie, I told you it doesn't bother me. I'm way over that now. Remember, the promise I made to you and to God?"

He placed a kiss on my forehead and held me in his arms for a minute. I was so thankful things had changed for him, but I did make a mental note to watch my alcohol intake and to not keep liquor in the house anymore. It really wasn't fair to Darius. I was going to stand in support of him and didn't want to have anything around the house that could tempt him.

Since we'd been back together, I was in a blissful place. It's funny how life takes you through some crazy things, only to bring you back full circle, but much better off than you were the first time around. A month ago, we weren't even speaking and now we were right back where we were before we broke up, but so much stronger and doing better than ever.

By 7:30, all the guests were there. Some of the ladies were playing spades at one table and the guys were playing dominos at another. The remaining group of women were sitting in the family room talking about everything from the latest book they'd read to the new gay guy working at the MAC store over at the mall. He could apply makeup and lashes better than a lot of the women working over there. There was music playing down in the basement and a few people were even dancing.

I heard the ping of a utensil on a glass in the family room as people began to make their way upstairs to the main level. Darius stood in the middle of the floor trying to get everyone's attention.

"Baby, what are you doing?" I asked.

"Can I have everyone's attention, please? I have something I'd like to say. As you all know by now, my Keisha and I are back together again."

A few positive remarks could be heard from various parts of the room.

"I have missed this woman every single day since the last time I saw her. There were days that I didn't know how I was gonna make it without her. We've been through the storm, but now we're back. Come here Keish."

I stood up and headed toward him. He placed his arm around my waist.

"Baby, you know how in love I am with you. When we first started dating, we were already talking about our future together. We talked about getting married and having a couple of babies. Then, I had to go away to take my position down in the ATL. I was excited about the opportunity because I'd waited for that transfer for years; six years to be exact. Remember how we talked about you relocating to be with me so we could build a life together?

"Yes, baby. I remember."

"Well, life happened. I left; you stayed. I started drinking even more than I was drinking before I left. I was drowning my sorrows in alcohol," he admitted. "I guess what I'm trying to say is, I really need you, Keisha. You are everything to me and I can't imagine having to live my life another day without you. I never knew that I could feel this way about anyone until I met you. My mornings don't start out right unless I can see your beautiful face; and my nights aren't complete without being able to kiss your lips before I go to bed."

He immediately got down on one knee. Pulling the ring box out of the pocket of his suit jacket, he grabbed my left hand.

"Keisha Ayanna Johnston, what I'm trying to ask is; will you marry me?"

There were gasps and sighs throughout the room. He took the four-carat princess cut diamond ring on a band of smaller diamonds from the box and placed it on my finger.

"Well, will you?"

"Yes! Darius, I will marry you!"

Looking at the beautiful ring he'd just placed on my finger, I began to cry. He held me close to him and we exchanged a kiss in front of all our friends and loved ones. I was so focused on what Darius was saying that I hadn't even noticed his Mom and Dad were now in the room.

"Come here, baby," Candice said, hugging me tightly. "I'm so happy to have you as my future daughter-in-law. I just want you two to always love each other and to be there through the thick and thin. I truly believe God created you for each other."

"Mom, thank you so much. I'm just glad things turned out the way God intended. We haven't done everything right; according to His plan, but we're really trying to do better."

Everyone was gathering around us to offer kind words and congratulations. This was by far the happiest day of my life and everyone dear to us was here to share it with us but my parents, although they called minutes later to offer congratulations as well. Mom apologized for them not being able to make it, but would have been there had they not been in Aruba on vacation. Darius had spoken with them a few days prior to let them know what his intentions were and to get their blessing. He had hidden all of this from me very well. I now knew why Jamel's color scheme for the decorations was in the purple family. Because it's one of my favorite colors and knowing Darius, he wanted this to be all about me.

For the rest of the evening, Darius and I stayed close to each other. We made our rounds throughout the room talking to our friends and showing off my new engagement ring. There was nothing better than sharing this special occasion with our special friends and family. Reaching for my hand, he admired the ring. He was so proud of himself. I looked at it and thought what an amazing job he'd done. It was beautiful! I couldn't wait to see what type of wedding band he had in mind. When men thought about approaching me from now on, they'd have to take a step back because there'd be no question that I'm spoken for and that my husband loves me very much. I knew that even before he bought the ring; but everyone else would surely know it now if they didn't already.

Pam and Shawn finally admitted to being involved with the whole surprise along with Jamel. I was really surprised that Shawn hadn't let the cat out of the bag, because she was absolutely terrible at keeping secrets. If you wanted something to remain confidential, you didn't share it with her. Jamel and Pam wouldn't tell a soul if you asked them not to, but Shawn couldn't hold water. They already knew what the deal was when I called them the other night. I was the only one who didn't.

"Girl, I wanted to tell you so bad, but Darius made us promise that we wouldn't say a word. Once I saw the ring, I knew there was no way that you could know about this until the time was right. You've got a good man, Keisha. You guys; please treat each other right," said Pam. "Put God first in your relationship and everything else will follow."

"Keisha, you deserve all of the love that your heart can hold. You've both been through a lot, so always remember where you came from and how you got here. If you can do that, you'll be all right," said Shawn with tears in her eyes.

"I'm so happy for you, said Candice."

"Thank you so much," grabbing her neck to give her a big hug. "I love you both so much!"

"You know we got your back. Y'all need to set the date because we've got a wedding to plan!" Monica walked up and joined the conversation. "I knew y'all were gonna get back together when I saw you at the restaurant. Love was just plastered all over both of your faces. I told Jamel that night that it was just a matter of time and you two would be married. Honestly, I thought you were just gonna show up one day married or something anyway. The way y'all were looking at each other from across that dinner table, I thought you would have been married by the next day!"

"Girl, you're crazy!" Shawn told her.

"I'm serious! You should have seen 'em! I could barely enjoy my dessert because I was so busy watching them. Finally, Rico told me that I needed to mind my own business."

"Where is he anyway?" I asked.

"I don't know; I think he's outside on his cell phone or something. He said he needed to call his mother."

Shawn, Pam and I just looked at each other. We knew Rico was playing her. He was probably talking to one of his side chicks. Someone he met at the club. Well, it wasn't any of my business. I had my own man to be thinking about and wasn't about to waste one ounce of my time on Rico. Thinking of my baby and how happy he just made me; I excused myself from the conversation and went to take a seat next to him while he bragged to Jamel about how he picked out my ring.

I found out later that Jamel had actually told Darius that he would have him to deal with, if he ever hurt me again. The two of them were tight, but Jamel didn't take any mess when it came to me. He was really my best friend, even more so than Monica or Pam. We had so much history together. He knew where my heart was, but he also knew that my health concerns could turn into a problem if I didn't keep the stress down. So, because of that; he had a true heart to heart with Darius. It was then that he told Jamel what his plan was and the two of them jumped into action to arrange the surprise engagement party. It would be a day I would never forget.

11 MORE THAN LOVE

As I headed toward my office, the aroma of fresh flowers filled the hallway. My jaw dropped when I walked into what looked like the botanical gardens on a warm and sunny spring day. There were dozens on top of dozens of roses filling my entire office in shades of red, purple, yellow, white, and even my new favorite, hot pink. Taking an estimated guess, I settled on ten dozen. A few of my employees were hanging around the area when I walked in. Looking from one of them to the other, there were nothing but smirks on their faces.

"Where in the world did all these flowers come from?" I sniffed the pink ones while reaching for the card that was attached.

"We were hoping you'd be able to shed some light on this situation for us," said Tanya, my assistant. "They started arriving at 8:00 o'clock this morning and from multiple florists. Not just one.

I read the card out loud:

You are my beautiful flower
The only woman I'm thinking of
Can't wait to spend my life with you
I love you more than love!

I hope you have a wonderful day, and I can't wait to hold
you in my arms later!

Love Darius

"Awe, that is so sweet," I said as I put the card back into the envelope. "Well, since you're all here. I have some news to share with you. Darius and I got engaged over the weekend," holding my hand out so they could get a good look at my new engagement ring.

"Oh, my goodness! Girl, that is the biggest diamond I've ever seen! You're going to need a body guard just to walk around with that one!"

Tanya grabbed my hand, pretending to drop it because it was too heavy. She was so funny. When Darius and I broke up, Tanya and I spent hours just talking about where things went wrong. She had always been in our corner and was so excited that we were not only back together, but now engaged to be married. Like me, Tanya was a hopeless romantic. Unfortunately, she had yet to find her Mr. Right.

After reading the cards accompanying the other floral arrangements, Tanya and I determined that there were ten dozen all together. The ten dozen roses represented the number of months we'd dated. Darius was very sentimental about anniversaries and other milestones. It was something else that I loved about him. He never forgot an anniversary or a special accomplishment and would find little ways to let me know how special I was or how proud he was of me.

"Tanya picked up the yellow arrangement and held it close to her nose. You should have seen everybody looking. You know how women are. Every woman in this place must have thought they were getting flowers, but they were all for you," she said. You are such a lucky woman to have a man like that. He is definitely a keeper."

"He truly is a blessing to me. He really came back strong, didn't he? Why don't you put those yellow ones in your office?"

"Oh wow! Thanks!" she sniffed them again. "You got that right. He did come back strong. So, have you two decided on the big day?" She asked.

"I'm still trying to get used to being engaged, but truthfully, I was thinking about next June. I haven't spoken to him about it yet, though. I've always wanted to get married in June and I'm sure he won't object."

"That sounds good. That'll give you plenty of time to plan everything."

Immediately, my mind drifted off to the day Darius and I would become one in the presence of God, our friends and families. The mere thought of it was making me very emotional. There were so many things I wanted to do. I wanted to give him babies. At least two, but I also wanted to do some traveling before we brought babies into the marriage. Maybe after the first or second year would be a good time to start trying. So much had changed in such a short time that I thought it would be better for us to enjoy each other first. Maybe I was being selfish, and maybe God had another plan. If he did, I'd have to let him navigate what the future held for us; but in my mind one or two years sounded good.

"You guys, we've got a lot of work to do today, so let's

get to it," remembering that we were supposed to be working, the group disbursed to their assigned work areas.

I decided to move some of the flowers to different parts of the office. They were far too beautiful to keep to myself. As I reached for another dozen, my phone rang. It was Darius.

"Hey, baby," I said. "Thank you so much for all of the flowers. They're beautiful! Did you write all of the poems that were attached all by yourself?"

"You know I did. I know some of them are a little corny. By the time I got to the fifth or sixth dozen, I started running out of rhyming words." We both laughed. "All jokes aside; you know I believe in showering you with beautiful things. You're my bride to be, so our bond is now even stronger than ever. I was hoping you had time this evening to join me for dinner right after work. I figured you could meet me at the house and we could just take one car."

"I think that can be arranged. What did you have in mind?"

"I was thinking about heading over to D.C. somewhere. Does that sound good? "That's where we went on our second date, remember?"

"Of course, I remember. It was only the second-best date I'd ever had," I told him.

"So, who took you on your best date?"

"My best date happened the day before when we went on that motorcycle ride. You remember the night we went to Gee's Spot to listen to jazz and have dinner? After dinner, you insisted on taking the motorcycle out."

"You're so crazy. Yes, I remember it like it was yesterday. We took that thing over one hundred miles per hour," he reminisced.

"I'm not sure how fast we were going, but my eyes were closed the entire time. I was holding on for dear life! The craziest thing about that ride is that I felt safe with you. It also gave me a chance to hold onto you. I could feel your six pack as I wrapped my arms around your chest. You didn't know it, but I wanted you. There was something sexy about that ride," I admitted.

"Yeah, I definitely remember it, just like it was yesterday, babe. I knew you wanted me too! You kept bringing your body close to me. Truth be told, I wanted to take you in the woods and bend you over my bike, but I was trying to be a gentleman. Plus, I knew you were a keeper and I didn't want to disrespect you because you didn't seem like the type that would do something like that. Little did I know, you were one of those freaky church girls," Darius let out a chuckle.

The two of us reminisced about the past for several more minutes before ending the call. I had a lot of work to do if I was going to get out of there in time to meet him for dinner. I still had multiple reviews to go, and wanted to finish up so I wouldn't have to think about it anymore. They all needed to be completed in three days, but I was already two thirds of the way through. If I didn't get started now, it might be 5:00 o'clock before I finished and I wanted to leave at 4:00 which would allow me enough time to get home and get sexy before dinner.

The day progressed without incident. I managed to get done by 3:00, so I was ahead of schedule. I'm sure everyone would be pleased with their evaluations and salary increases, though some would be more pleased than others. I had a lot of overachievers on my team. There were some who were star performers and some who were doing just a little more than enough to get by, but each one of them brought something unique to the team. For that, I wouldn't trade either one of them.

I left the office at 4:15, headed home to shower and

change into something less business appropriate and more date with my fiancé appropriate. I wanted to get his attention as soon as he laid eyes on me. I decided on an electric blue wrap dress I'd been dying to wear for him. It showed a little cleavage and hugged my curves in all the right places. Looking in the mirror, as I held it against my body, I was pleased and knew Darius would be too. The only other time I'd worn it, I received so many compliments that I bought one in another color.

Darius had a habit of selecting unique and romantic places to take me to. I knew tonight would be no different, so I wanted to be ready. He'd been trying to take me into DC for about a week now, so I knew that was the direction we were going in tonight even before I asked him.

While showering, I couldn't help but thank God for being so good to me. He sent Darius back and things were never going to be the same for either of us. We were getting married! I still couldn't believe it. In about a year and a half, we would be married. The very thought of being Mrs. Darius Kingston made my heart warm. We were going to have a very good life together. Keisha Kingston had a very nice ring to it and I vowed to stay true to the man and the name forever. I would need to start making the arrangements very soon. At least secure the venue.

While waiting for Darius, my mind wandered to our future. I could see us in our wedding attire with my girls in beautiful purple or blackberry colored dresses. Maybe I should step outside of my comfort zone and go with something a little brighter for the summer season since I want to get married in June. I envisioned myself in a beautiful form fitting gown with a low cut back. I had so much work ahead of me and would need to get started right after the Christmas holidays. Luckily, Pam and Shawn were good at that type of thing and I'm certain they would be happy to help me bring it all together. Who needs a wedding planner when you have them? Monica had even volunteered to help. Lately, she'd been spending so much time with Rico that no one heard much from her, but who was I to judge? I was spending most of my time with Darius. Thinking like my mother, she would tell me to hire a wedding planner. Who was I fooling? I would weigh my options very soon. I put a note on my calendar to make an appointment at the Gaylord Hotel to discuss using one of the ballrooms for our reception. I also made a note to research the trip to St. Thomas for our honeymoon. Darius was pulling into the driveway, so I gave myself another glance in the mirror before grabbing my purse and coat, before heading out the door.

12 ANYTHING FOR YOU

We arrived at Fiola Mare's on K Street at 6:30. Keisha and I had always enjoyed the atmosphere here. After dinner, we usually took a walk down by the water, a drive around D.C. or a romantic walk on the mall. There was a Victoria's Secret on the way and we would stop there so Keisha could pick out some sexy little things for me to enjoy later. Sometimes, the sales associates would let me sit outside her dressing room so I could give her the thumbs up, which I always did. Keisha looked good in everything she put on. I had never seen her wearing anything that didn't suit her beautiful figure, but she always wanted my opinion anyway. We'd have to head over there after dinner tonight.

While walking toward the restaurant, I reached for her soft, clammy hand and pulled her closer. The warmth of her body turned me on so much that I wanted to take her back to the car and make love to her right in the back seat. Too bad we hadn't driven the Range Rover, because I might have tried it. The BMW was a little small for that. There was always so much passion between us, I could get excited just by accidentally brushing up against her. The truth is, her smile even aroused me; especially when I looked at those dimples. I was addicted to them and couldn't get enough. Because of it, I made sure she was smiling as much as possible.

"What are you smiling about?" She asked.

"I was just thinking about how much I love you."

"I love you too, Baby Cakes." There were those dimples again. *If she keeps this up, I won't even be able to make it through dinner. She just called me Baby Cakes. She hadn't called me that since we first started dating, the first time.*

"So, why did you want to come here? This isn't just an everyday place. This is one of those places you visit on special occasions." She joked.

"Well, it is a special occasion, isn't it? We did just get engaged. Last night, we were surrounded by so many people that we couldn't enjoy any private time. So, I thought a post engagement celebration was a good idea. What better place could we have come to on our second day as an engaged couple than the place we came to on our second date?"

"You are so corny," she joked. "I love that about you. We're going to have so many things to celebrate next year, aren't we? I'm going to have to make sure I record these anniversaries so nothing slips by me. You're going to have a lot of anniversary gifts to buy if you keep this up."

I knew she was serious. But then, she also knew I would be doing that anyway. It was nothing for me to buy her something I knew she wanted just because. In fact, I'd ordered her a diamond necklace this morning at the jeweler. I didn't even know what the occasion would be. I suppose just one of those "just because" moments.

The waitress guided us to a very romantic table for two, tucked away in a far corner of the restaurant. There were only two other couples sitting in our section, and one of them appeared to be finishing up because they already had the check. So, we had lots of privacy. The flicker of the candles placed on each of the tables illuminated the entire room just enough for us to see each other, but not too much to kill the ambience.

"This is really nice, isn't it?" she said, squeezing my hand tightly.

Staring at her from across the table, I couldn't help but think about how beautiful she was. I couldn't wait to have children with this woman. A little girl that looked just like her was what I desired most of all. I wanted to have another son too, but I really wanted her to give birth to our daughter first.

"Baby, that's a beautiful dress you're wearing. The color is so perfect on you and goes great with your complexion."

"I was beginning to think you hadn't noticed."

"What is that, royal blue? It's beautiful, but not as beautiful as you."

"Thanks, baby. It's actually called electric blue."

"You're looking pretty good too, with your fine self."

"Why thank you, my love," I smiled. "I guess we just make a very good-looking couple, huh?"

"You got that right, babe."

Suddenly, my mind wandered to the future. I could see us sitting across from each other just like we were at this moment; but we are now much older. Keisha has salt and pepper colored hair and my mustache and goatee are all gray. She is still the most beautiful woman I've ever seen. In my vision, we're in our sixties and I still can't wait to get her home and make love to her in the most passionate way. Will I still be able to perform like I do now? I sure hope so. Wow, what a strange thought.

The waitress came over to take our drink order before disappearing to the bar. I had gotten into the habit of drinking cranberry juice and ginger ale since I'd stopped drinking. Keisha ordered the same.

"Baby, you sure you don't want a glass of wine?"

"No, I'm fine. I'm standing in support of you, babe."

"I told you that I was fine. Really, if you want something, go ahead and order it. It's fine with me. I can handle it."

"I'm good. You know I was never a drinker anyway, so I'm cool. Trust me. Besides, I decided last night that I was going to stop too. I don't need it. We can have an alcohol-free relationship, marriage, and household."

"So, how was work?"

"It was good. I finally finished writing all those reviews. How about you?"

"We made it through the equipment inspection. The inspectors should be on their way to LaGuardia Airport right now to perform the same tests."

She always seemed so interested in my work and loved to come out to the tower while we were directing the air traffic. She said it turned her on to watch me in action doing what I do. She was always so cute, because she'd try to remember some of the Air Traffic Controller terminology.

"By the way, I'm off on Thursday. What's your schedule?"

"I'm on that day from 7:30 – 5:30, why? What's up?"

"I was thinking about coming up for lunch. Is that okay?"

"Yeah, baby. Anytime you want to come up for lunch is fine with me."

"You want me to order something?"

"No, I'll take care of it."

"Sounds like a date to me. Can you be there by 1:30?"

"I sure can. Thanks, baby."

"Why are you thanking me? I told you, you're welcome there any time. You're my baby and all the guys around there already know that. They have no problem with you coming through. Their wives all do it."

We enjoyed our dinner and even ordered Watermelon and Kiwi Sorbet for dessert. We fed each other until both dishes were empty. I moved to her side of the table so that we were sitting side by side. We sat there holding hands while waiting for the check. I rubbed my hand up and down her right thigh until both of her legs were exposed. She wasn't wearing any pantyhose. My breathing became heavy as I felt the warmth of her against my hand. I wanted to touch her again, but there was still another couple sitting nearby and I was also trying to be good. The rise and fall of her chest indicated she was feeling the same thing. I caught myself and tried to pull back.

"What part of the game is this? Oh, is that how you're going to do me?" she smirked.

"It's okay, babe. Wait until I get you home tonight," I said.

I liked to keep her aroused. By the time we made it home, she'd be out of that dress before I closed the front door. Ready and anticipating what would happen next. I had it all planned out. Still, in my mind I knew that we should wait until we got married; but we had already gone so far.

"Baby, have you been putting much thought into setting the wedding date?" I asked to change the subject.

"Well, now that you mentioned it, yes I have," she replied in as calm a manner as she could. She was trying to play the game.

"Well, what's it going to be, future Mrs. Kingston?"

"What do you think about next June? That will give me enough time to plan my dream wedding."

"Baby, if that's what you want, then that's what it'll be.

I'll mark two weeks off my calendar when I get to work tomorrow. What about the honeymoon?"

"I was thinking about that too, and I was wondering if you'd like to go to St. Thomas? I would love to go there again."

"Your wish is my command. So, it looks like a wedding in June and a trip to St. Thomas immediately following the wedding. Maybe I better take three weeks off," I said.

"Keisha, you have made me the happiest man alive. I have so much to be thankful for. You can't even imagine how thankful I am that God answered all my prayers. I keep having flashbacks of standing on my balcony in Atlanta; begging God to bring you back to me. Never even thinking that He was listening. When you weren't there, I thought I was being punished for something. What I finally realized and I know I've heard it many times before is God answers prayers in His time. I wanted what I wanted and I wanted it in my time. I know that it doesn't work that way and it was a wakeup call for me. I'm just so thankful that I was patient, and didn't give up."

"I know what you mean. I was being very stubborn when you called me this past summer. All I could think about was the hurt I would feel if I saw you. That's why I kept blocking you out. I just couldn't handle all the hurt being brought back to the surface. I knew if I saw you, I wouldn't be able to control what I was feeling. When you asked me to meet you at the beach for the weekend, I really wanted to come. I was just afraid, Darius."

"Keisha, we're okay. We're finally okay. So, let's not live in the past. We've got so many happy memories to build upon from this day forward. Let's think about those things instead."

"You're right. Let's leave the past in the past."

We agreed that we wouldn't dwell too much on what

had been, but what was to come. That was all that mattered now. Our upcoming wedding was the priority. Making my beautiful bride the happiest woman alive was my priority and I was not going to fail at that. I wanted to do so much for her.

13 PRIVATE ROOM

I was going to surprise Darius with a picnic lunch today at the tower. He had been working so hard lately, that I wanted to make sure he was eating a proper lunch. I pulled the picnic basket from the pantry and loaded it with the bowl of chicken salad I'd made earlier that morning along with turkey & roast beef sliced wafer thin just like he liked it. I packed several slices of wheat and white bread, provolone cheese, a small jar of mayonnaise, mustard and pickles and a bottle of sparkling cider. I made half a dozen deviled eggs and some freshly baked chocolate chip cookies. I added a small container of fresh strawberries and whipped cream along with fresh carrots, broccoli, and cauliflower. Finally, I put in napkins, a table cloth, plastic ware and glasses. I slipped into a charcoal grey Donna Karan sweater and a black mini skirt; not too short. I always made sure that I looked my best when going to his job because I wanted to represent him well, always. A glance in the mirror confirmed that my wardrobe selection was a good choice, and appropriate for the occasion.

I put the picnic basket in the back seat of the car and headed toward the airport.

"Hey, baby. I just wanted to let you know that I was on my way."

"Okay, Sweetheart. I'll see you in a little while. I love you."

"I love you too."

While driving to the airport, I couldn't help but daydream about the wedding plans. I had picked up a copy of *Bride Magazine* yesterday, but hadn't gotten a chance to look at it yet. I envisioned myself in an elegant ivory colored wedding gown; nothing traditional at all. The dress in my vision had spaghetti straps with a cowl front to expose a little cleavage. The straps crossed in the back several times over to secure the dress that has a bare back all the way down to the waistline. Perhaps something with lace and rhinestones with a lot of skin showing through, but not too much to be inappropriate for a church. I can see Darius standing at the alter waiting for me to get there. He's smiling the biggest smile I have ever seen, but has tears in his eyes just the same. Our wedding day is going to be the most beautiful day ever. It was all I could think about lately and I was so excited.

Stopping at the gate to the tower entrance, I pressed the buzzer to let security know I was there. The picnic basket was heavy, so I was glad to find a front parking space. Darius was watching from the window, so I knew he would meet me before I reached the building.

"Hey, baby girl." He leaned forward, kissing my lips. "Let me carry that basket for you. What did you do, pack the whole kitchen? This thing is heavy!"

"A few of your favorite things," I teased. "I figured you could share with the guys after I leave if you want to."

"That was very considerate of you. I'm sure they'll appreciate it."

94

"Well, I would like for you and me to find a quiet little corner somewhere around here so we can have some privacy. You think that would be possible?"

"I think there's an open office up there. You don't have to worry about anyone disturbing our lunch because everyone else is on station and will be working at least until I get back from lunch. Plus, I already told them not to disturb me."

"That sounds good. Show me the way and I'll get it all set up."

I spread the checkered table cloth out on the small office table. There were two candles still in the basket from the last romantic lunch we'd shared; so, I lit them and placed them on the table too. I placed all the items out so Darius could eat what he wanted. I was actually getting a little hungry myself.

"Keish, this looks great! What did I do to deserve this?"

"Just being the best fiancé a woman could ever ask for qualifies you." I kissed his lips slowly. "I just wanted to thank you for loving me so much."

"Baby, you don't have to thank me for that. You are my entire world; and I would love you no matter what."

"Wow, baby! If I didn't know better, I'd think you hadn't eaten all week. Have I been starving you or something? I just watched you put away a chicken salad sandwich, turkey and cheese sandwich, pickles, four deviled eggs, strawberries and cheese, and three chocolate chip cookies."

"I know, right? Everything is so good! I'm so lucky to have a woman like you. You're beautiful and you can throw some food together too! The guys are probably up there right now hatin' because they know I'm down here getting all the attention."

"Thanks. If you're all done, would you mind taking the

leftovers to them so they can eat? I'd hate to see all this stuff go to waste. There should be enough left for everyone."

"I can do that. I'll be right back. Do you need me to get you anything?"

"No, I'm good."

Watching him walk away, all I could do was smile. I was the happiest woman alive and I absolutely adored that man. While waiting for him to return, my mind wandered back to our love making session last night. I was getting excited just thinking about it. From the mere thought of his hand on my leg at the restaurant excited me so much that I couldn't wait to get home. We never even made it to the bedroom. We went from the sofa to the floor in front of the fireplace before we made it to our final resting spot in the bedroom. By then, we were both so exhausted that we passed out.

"Come here and give your man a hug," Darius said, pulling me from my seat.

I could feel the warmth of his body through my sweater as soon as our bodies touched.

"Babe, I don't know what's wrong with me. I've been consumed with thoughts that are not right! A lot more lately than ever. I'm not sure what to do with myself."

"I know exactly what you mean. I've been trying to go about things differently this time. I have so much respect for you. Not that I didn't the first time, but I was so selfish I thought more about myself and what I wanted. Now I'm trying to think more about what's right for us."

"You've really been thinking about that?"

"Keisha, I can't stop thinking about it. I know how things are supposed to be. I've always known it. I've damaged you. You used to be a good girl and now I have you doing things that you would never have done before. In the eyes of God, we both know it's not right, but we keep doing it. God is not through with either us. We're both a work in progress. I just want to do right by you. I want us to be able to sit in church and know that we're living right. Right now, we can't do that."

"Awe, Darius. That is really sweet. I love you too, babe. I'm going to try harder to keep my mind off the things that we shouldn't be doing; at least until after we get married. I'll try, but I can't promise you anything. Agreed?"

"Agreed. This has never been me, but for you, I'm going to do my absolute best. I love you just that much. I told you, I was going to make an honest woman out of you. We're going to do what pleases God and not ourselves. It's what's right."

"I better get out of here, so you can get back to work. Thanks for letting me steal you away for a little while."

"No, thank you for bringing lunch. You look beautiful, if I didn't already say it."

As I walked away, I couldn't help but get excited about the fact that he was going to be my husband soon. I was really going to be spending the rest of my life with him and I couldn't believe it was really happening. There was a time when I thought I'd never see him again. Now, all I could think about was waking up next to him every morning and growing old together. He was changing right before my eyes, and I liked what I was seeing.

"I love you, Darius. Oh, and don't forget the picnic basket tonight," I reminded him.

"I got you. I love you!" he yelled before heading back into the building after I was safely in my car.

14 THE MEETING

After work, Darius came straight to my place to change his clothes. He had to make it to an Alcoholics Anonymous meeting by 7:30 and he was running late.

"Baby, I want to ask you something," I followed him through the bedroom trying to help him find something more comfortable to change into.

"What is it, babe?"

"I was wondering if I could go with you to your meeting tonight."

Looking at me through the bathroom mirror, he stopped wiping his face with the towel.

"Keisha, you don't have to do that."

"Darius, I want to. I'm your fiancé now, and I need to know what's going on in your life. I've never been to one of them since you started going and I think it's time. I don't even know what I'm expecting to happen, but I just want you to know that I support you through this one hundred percent. I want everyone to know that you have people who love you."

"That's the nicest thing I've heard in a while. No one has ever volunteered to go to an AA meeting with me. When things are going well, there are tons of people who want to celebrate with you; when you're popping bottles, and getting messed up. But, when you fall, those same people are nowhere to be found. There've been times through this whole ordeal that I felt totally alone," he admitted. "I'm glad you're in my corner."

"Yes baby, I'm here now and I really need to do this not only for you, but for me. We're going to be married soon, and not only is it my duty to be there for you; but it's an honor for me to help you through all of this," I admitted.

"Darius, I don't know if I told you, but I'm so proud of you. Even when things were at the lowest point in our relationship, I never looked down on you. I've had a hard time verbalizing it since the first time around. I just want you to know that you've always been my giant; even when you didn't feel as big or as strong as a giant yourself. You've always been that to me. I know I'm stubborn and it seemed easy for me to let the relationship go, but in my heart, I missed you like crazy. The stubborn part of me wouldn't let me reach out to you even though I wanted to so many nights. For that, I apologize. Just remember, to me you've always been ten feet tall."

"Wow. I never knew you felt like that about me." With tears in his eyes, he held me close to his chest. "I'm so glad you told me. As far as you going to the meeting with me, I would be so happy to have you there. Thank you."

"Well, I guess we'd better get going then," grabbing our coats, we hurried out the door.

Darius held my hand as we drove to the meeting in silence. Without even saying so, I knew he needed me to be there for him. I knew at that moment I would need to attend the meetings at least once a week to keep him encouraged. More often than that, if he needed me to. He was doing such a great job at staying sober that I wanted to make sure he knew that everyone was pulling for him whether they said so or not. I adored him. Each day that Darius made it through and stayed sober was a major accomplishment for him. I often wondered if he thought about the alcohol or even craved it, even though he said he didn't. I would never want him to have a moment of weakness, and feel like he couldn't talk to me about it. I wanted to be his biggest supporter.

Instantly, I thought about growing up in an alcoholic household. Both of my parents had stopped drinking many years ago, but it was a terrible thing to watch as a young girl. I was so thankful they had both been delivered from the disease; and yes, that is what it is. My father had been sober for over twenty years, but I remember the fights they used to have. My mother didn't become an alcoholic until much later, but she'd also been sober for ten years now. I thanked God that I had never become a victim of alcohol or drugs. Knowing it was in my blood line caused me to stay as far away from it as possible because I knew the potential was always there for me to become dependent on either drugs or alcohol. Though, I did enjoy an occasional glass of wine with dinner or at social gatherings, I didn't have to have it. If it would make Darius's journey easier, I wasn't going to take another drink. It just seemed like the right thing to do.

We took our seats in the meeting room alongside people from all walks of life. The couple sitting to our left, Marie and John had been married for over thirty years. Marie recently discovered John had been fired from his job because of his drinking. He was a Federal Government employee making almost $200K a year and now he was jobless because he let the drinking consume his entire life. Marie admitted they used to socialize a lot with friends, and always had a fully stocked liquor cabinet in the basement. Once John admitted he had a problem and vowed to stop drinking, she said things became much worse instead of better. John would conceal alcohol in old 7-Eleven cups to make her think that he was drinking soda. She said he would empty Mountain Dew from the bottle and fill it with liquor. While watching a movie, he would sit there and nurse the bottle of what she thought was soda, until he eventually passed out. Marie began to cry when she told the group that their marriage was on the verge of ending because of all of this.

"Keisha, is this your first time in an AA meeting?" asked Caroline, the group counselor.

"Yes, this is my first meeting."

"Did you come here with expectations of what might happen?" she asked.

"No. I came here because I didn't know what to expect, but I knew I needed to be here for Darius. We recently became engaged and I felt it was important to experience this part of his life . . our lives. He's made a lifetime commitment to being sober and I support him in it one hundred percent."

"I'd like everyone to know that my baby came here on her own free will. I didn't want her to come, but when she asked me I knew I had to agree. Once I told her she could come, I realized how much I really needed her here. This woman is my entire world and her presence here means absolutely everything to me," Darius kissed my hand and held it close to his heart.

"That's really sweet, Keisha. Darius did announce the engagement in another meeting. He's talked about you so much, we feel like we already know you. It's very important for loved ones to be a part of these meetings. There's a lot of energy that goes into dealing with family members who are suffering from alcoholism and other addictions," said Caroline. "It can be emotionally exhausting. Does anyone else have anything to add?"

There was silence throughout the room. Christopher, a young man of about 22 or so sat with his head in his hands.

"Would it be okay if I left a little early tonight? I have to get up extra early tomorrow and my drive back home is over an hour," Christopher said.

"Yes, you can leave when we take our break. Before you go, I'll need to get a sample from you," she handed Christopher a plastic cup in a plastic bag. He knew what to do with it. Christopher left the room headed for the restroom and returned with his urine sample just minutes later with a man who looked like some sort of security guard trailing closely behind him. I couldn't help but wonder if he washed his hands. Was it normal to have to give urine samples at an AA meeting? I'd never heard of that before, but this was my first visit so maybe it was. I would have to ask Darius about that later.

There was a young lady falling asleep in the corner of the room. Chanelle had been silent for the entire meeting.

"Chanelle, would you like to join us?" Caroline teased.

"Not really, Miss Caroline. It's been a long day and I'm tired. I can't wait to get out of here."

Darius later told me that Chanelle was a recovering sex addict and an alcoholic. She had been ordered to attend these meetings because she was caught in the men's room at work having sex with one of the CEOs of the company. Chanelle would get wasted at work and start sleeping with anyone who would pay attention to her. She confessed to having oral sex in the supply room and multiple sexual encounters in various places throughout the building with different men who worked there, all in efforts to boost her career. She said she'd also had a threesome in the lounge after mostly everyone had gone home for the evening. She admitted to being propositioned by the security guard who had witnessed the encounter on one of the cameras. He told

Chanelle he would keep his silence if she had oral sex with him after work one day. She said she agreed to do it, but he told anyway.

Needless to say, the security guard was terminated. Chanelle would have been fired also had she not admitted that she needed help and then followed through with counseling and other medical help. Once I found out that she was only 23 years old, my heart ached for her. She had grown up without a father and was obviously looking for love in all the wrong places. I couldn't help but wonder what happened to the CEO she slept with? It always seemed like the ones higher up the ladder were the ones to get away free and clear.

During the remainder of the meeting, we all talked about what we would be doing during the Christmas Holiday that would be different from other years when the addictions were controlling our lives. Darius and I would be spending it together, planning our wedding. We would probably spend some time with our friends and family and maybe go on a long weekend getaway or something. I was really just excited to be spending it with him. It didn't matter what we did. DJ was spending the school year in California with Denise and wouldn't be out for a visit until spring break. It looked like we could do what we wanted.

Attending holiday functions was always fun, but this year was different. I didn't mind being shut in with Darius, spending quality time. Just the two of us. Besides, we had some lost time to make up for. Now that he wasn't jaded by the alcohol, he was so different. Even emotional sometimes. I told the group that I was just so thankful to have him back in my life with no alcohol involved, that I didn't care what we did as long as we were together.

At the end of the meeting, everyone stayed around to chat for a few minutes. Several people came up to me to say how good Darius and I were for each other. They thought we made a beautiful couple and gave us many blessings for a happy marriage. Caroline told me how much Darius had spoken of me in the meetings. She seemed to know an awful lot about me, but Darius was a proud man. I'm sure he'd shared some of our fondest memories with her.

"The love he has for you is real, young lady. It's rare to hear a man speak of a woman the way Darius speaks about you," she said. "You two have something very special. Have a great evening."

"And you as well, Caroline. It was a pleasure to meet you."

Caroline continued with good-byes to some of the other meeting participants and visitors. She was going to have to wake Chanelle because she was fast asleep in the back of the room.

"Baby, thank you for coming to this meeting with me," Darius said as we were leaving the building. "I thought I was okay doing this on my own, but I really do need you more than you know."

"Sweetie, I told you I'm here for you no matter what. Ride or die, remember? I mean that."

"Ride or die," he said.

He grabbed my hand, holding it during the entire ride back home. I would never leave Darius this time. You see, he showed me what it truly meant to love someone unconditionally. He loved me that way from the very beginning, but I turned my back on him when he needed me the most. I would always regret that, but I also believed we had to go through what we went through to get to where we are now. We had grown so much and now we both had so much love to give to each other and prayerfully, a lifetime in which to give it. I know, Darius wanted me to leave the past in the past but it hurt so much; and now we're here.

I suppose I was just trying to remember where we came from and because things were now so good, I couldn't help but rejoice at it all. Unfortunately, to do that, forced me to remember some of the more challenging times that I now realized were lessons that we could turn into opportunities to do better.

15 SIDE HUSTLE

Latoya and her bridal party were all ready to have their faces made up by the time I arrived at the Ritz-Carlton Hotel. The contract required me to be set up and be ready to go 30 minutes prior to the appointment. I was scheduled for 11:00 and it was currently 10:30. Latoya was a very pretty young lady without make-up, so I was certain that I wouldn't be doing too much to her today. She was a natural beauty and while I understood her desire to be all made up for her wedding day, I would make sure she didn't look like a drag queen about to take the stage. Instead, a beautiful, blushing bride would suit her better.

There were four bridesmaids, the maid of honor, and matron of honor requiring my services. The dresses were a beautiful olive green shade, which was a perfect choice for the season. Before seeing it, I couldn't envision what it would look like, but seeing them all together; they looked beautiful. Her bridesmaids were women of color in all shades, the olive green looked beautiful against their skin.

Latoya was a bridesmaid from another wedding I'd worked the previous year. Now it was her turn. That day, she continued to compliment my work and asked if she could hire me for her wedding. She was paying $175 for each member of the bridal party and $250 for herself, which was a very good rate for just a couple of hours of work, and touchups prior to the reception.

"Keisha, my girls look gorgeous!" said Latoya.

"Thanks. Well, it's your turn now," I told her.

Making up Latoya's face was really the easiest of them all because her skin was flawless. Her even skin tone made her face the perfect palette for the most beautiful colors. MAC's NW40 liquid foundation suited her skin tone perfectly, and it was lighter than most foundations so she wouldn't look like she had makeup caked on. I used lashes that made her look like she had naturally long ones without being overdramatic. I used earth tones like amber lights, mulch, and rice paper eye shadows with just a hint of olive green. She wasn't a lipstick wearer so I decided to use a lip gloss in a sheer color called U-turn and a lip glass for added shine. Antonio would be reduced to tears when he saw her coming down the aisle.

I stayed through the ceremony and did touch ups prior to the photographs to disguise any tear-stained cheeks or running mascara from the crying bridesmaids and the bride as well. Once they were about to enter the reception, I made my exit. Latoya's mother handed me an envelope and I headed out the door.

I would use this money as the down payment for some of my own wedding expenses. In fact, I had enough appointments on my calendar to pay for our wedding and the reception if I planned well, and wouldn't have to use any of my regular salary. After seeing LaToya's wedding and the beautiful reception hall set up, I knew it was time for me to get the ball rolling on my own event. First thing tomorrow.

16 STEPHANIE

I hurried home to find Darius on the phone. As I opened the front door, he quickly disconnected the line.

"Hi, Baby. Who was that?"

"Oh, just someone I hadn't spoken to in a while. I told her that we had gotten engaged."

"So, who is someone, and why am I just hearing about her?"

"She's the woman I briefly dated before you and I reunited. The one I told you about. She's been calling my cell phone again lately, so I thought I needed to answer so I could let her know you and I are back together and not to call anymore."

"So, she knew about us?"

"Keisha, anybody who would listen knew about us. Her name is Stephanie, and I made it very clear to her that you were the woman I wanted to be with. I told her that I couldn't get into a serious relationship with her back in Atlanta because my heart and soul belonged to you. Of course, she didn't understand how I could be carrying a torch for someone in hopes of reuniting someday, but it wasn't for her to understand. I knew what was in my heart. I actually wish I'd never met her," he admitted.

"How many times has she called? This is the first time I've heard her name."

"She's called about six times in the past week alone. I never told you her name. I just said that I'd dated someone. Anyway, when I told her we were back together and were now engaged, she flipped out. She told me that she was going to make me see that she was the woman for me, and not you."

"What? So, what are you going to do about her? She sounds like a stalker to me."

Well, I changed my voicemail already. If that doesn't work, I'm going to change my number. Maybe I need to just do that anyway."

"What do you mean you changed your voicemail?"

"Why don't you call the number and find out."

I picked up the phone and dialed his number. He ended the call so it would go straight to his voice mail.

"Hello, this is Darius. I've recently been reunited with my soulmate. Her name is Keisha and we're planning to spend the rest of our lives together. Please don't make problems for us by calling. Keisha, baby? If this is you, I'll see you later tonight. I love you."

"Darius, I can't believe you put that on your voicemail. That is so sweet; in an odd sort of way!"

"Baby, I'll do anything to get you to understand how serious I am about our future together. I'm not going to jeopardize it by letting someone from my past interfere. My love belongs to you and you alone and if I have to write it in the sky from an airplane, I'll do just that. Well, I might not be flying the plane, but I'll get it done. Keisha, I won't lie by saying I didn't have friends while we were apart. I can promise you that anyone who was my friend knew about you. Some of them wanted more than friendship. My only regret is having sex with Stephanie the one time that I did. I wish I had saved my body for you instead of giving in to sexual temptation."

"It's okay, baby. I'm not innocent either, remember? I was involved intimately with Brian a couple times. I wish I'd waited too, but neither of us did. We didn't know we would actually end up back here. All we can do from this point on is not let anything like that happen again. I admit I'm a little disappointed that she's calling. Men don't do stupid stuff like that, but women are something else. We're back together and getting married in a year and a half. We're committed to each other and that's it."

"Yes, we are. Thank you for understanding."

"I'm cool with it. One thing though; if she keeps calling, let me know so I can handle her. Ride or die, remember?"

"That's my girl! I would never put you in harm's way, but I'm glad you have my back just the same."

Yes, I did have his back and would definitely have a conversation with this woman if she didn't back off. Darius had already told her and now she was being down right disrespectful. I loved him more than anything and would come to his defense if I had to. She'd stop calling once I was finished with her. If she continued even after hearing his voicemail, she was giving me an invitation to step to her anyway. I'd just wait to see what she did next before deciding how to deal with her.

"I love you, baby."

"I love you too; but you'll need to change that voicemail in a few days. I wouldn't want any of your colleagues to hear it. Oh, and another thing? Don't wait so long to tell me what's going on the next time. I should have known that she was calling after the first call."

"Yes, you're right, babe. I just didn't want to make you upset. And don't even worry about that voicemail. The guys from work all call me on the work cell phone anyway, but if they did hear it; I'm not ashamed." He gave me a tender kiss and held me tightly in his arms.

17 WHERE'S MONICA?

Shawn, Pam and I had made a date for lunch after church today. We decided to go to a Japanese Steak House, agreeing that this was the best choice considering we were all trying to get into better shape for before the wedding.

"Girl, have you picked out your wedding dress yet?" asked Pam.

"I have some ideas, but I haven't committed to anything up to this point. Why, have you seen something?"

"I've been skimming through a few of the bridal magazines to see if there was anything that would suit you, but so far I haven't seen anything. It has to be perfect, I do know that. Have you thought much about what color we're gonna wear?"

"Yes, I have. I've been thinking about either blackberry or persimmon. It's like a real deep burnt orange color. I just think it'll look good for a summer wedding. Blackberry would look good for an evening wedding. I'm sort of leaning more toward that. They have the color over at David's Bridal and I've seen it on line on some of the designers' web sites. It's pretty to me, but you guys can tell me what you think. We should be able to find a dress that complements all of you in that color. I know this is going to sound very vain and maybe even a little shallow, but I'm so glad you all have sexy figures. You're sure to look good in any style dress we choose. I want to see you guys in something strapless or a halter style dress. That's what I envision, but I guess it depends on what style dress I choose for myself. I would like them to complement each other. Anyway, I made an appointment at the bridal shop over on Pennsylvania Avenue for two weeks from today so we can start sorting out the details. Will that work for you two? I can always reschedule the date if I need to.

"It sure will. I'm excited about this and can't wait to see how the colors work out and the dresses too," said Shawn, putting a forkful of shrimp and stir fried vegetables in her mouth.

"Oh, I almost forgot. Guess what happened yesterday?"

"What?" Pam asked.

"One of Darius's old friends called. Apparently, she's been blowing up his cell phone for the past week or so. I guess she can't handle the fact that we're back together."

"What in the heck is her problem? Let me know if you need me. You know we got your back," said Pam with so much attitude, I could almost see her in a cat fight with this Stephanie woman.

"She's gonna make me put on my ninja gear and wait outside of her house," she added.

"It's okay. First of all, she lives all the way down in Atlanta. You should hear the message he put on his voicemail to discourage her and anyone else from his past from continuing to call. It's very sweet and heart felt."

"You know how Darius is. He's in love with you! I don't believe there's anything he wouldn't do to prove his love for you. Come on now; look at the diamond on your finger. The thing is huge!" Shawn grabbed my hand to get a better look at the ring. "He hooked you up with that one. It is absolutely beautiful!"

"He sure did," Pam chimed in.

"Have either of you heard from Monica lately?"

"I heard she's been hanging out with Rico just about every day. I'm still shocked she decided to date a stripper. You know how conservative Monica is. Rico must have really put it on her, because we don't see her like we used to. He's got that chick on lock!"

"I'm surprised by that too. I mean, you know he must be sleeping with a lot of those women who come to the club. Rico does a lot of private parties and I'd be willing to bet money that some of them would pay to sleep with him too," said Shawn. "In fact, I know a girl who goes to the same nail salon I go to. I overheard her a couple of months ago talking about him. He had done a private party for her and a couple of her girlfriends. From the tone of the conversation, she's not just a fan."

"Better her than me. There's no way in the world I'm going to be in a relationship with a man who dances for women for a living. Have you ever been to that club and seen the women all over those dancers?" Pam asked with a look of disgust on her face.

"I went there once. It was two years ago, and Monica wanted me to go there with her. It was my birthday and she just knew I would have a blast. It really wasn't my thing and I was ready to leave quick, fast and in a hurry! I must admit, there was this one dancer that might have gotten my attention had he not been a dancer. I'll never forget him. We were passing each other in a hallway that night and when our eyes met; there was such a connection that it almost took the wind out of me. I started feeling dizzy and everything! I felt like I was moving in slow motion like they do in those Spike

Lee movies! He was built! He had light brown eyes and long dreadlocks. That brother was fine! Keisha, you would have fallen in love the moment you saw his dreads, girl!" Shawn confessed.

"I think I remember you telling me about that. Would you have had sex with him if the opportunity presented itself?"

"No, I don't think I could have done that. Even using a condom, I would have been afraid. He definitely was eye candy, though."

"Well, all we can do is pray that she's protecting herself when she sleeps with him. How do we know that she's sleeping with him anyway?" asked Pam.

"Come on now! Have you seen Rico? He's not bad looking at all. He falls in the same class as that other one. He's eye candy too." Shawn said. "I mean, look at him. You know he must have it going on in the bedroom if he's a dancer. I'm sure he gets it in every chance he gets, too!"

"You're so nasty!" Pam said, turning her head in the opposite direction pretending to be disgusted again by Shawn's comments. She was the churchiest of the group.

"I'm just keepin' it real!"

Those two were always debating back and forth. Sometimes, I wondered how they stayed friends because they were both so opinionated. If Pam said it was green, Shawn would say it was blue. Sometimes I thought they did it intentionally, but at the end of the day, they had each other's backs. I knew back in the day, they would go to blows if anyone tried to do any harm to the other. In fact, they were that way about me too. In our adult lives, there were other ways to deal with drama when it needed to be dealt with. I would have to keep that in mind for Stephanie, if she didn't back off.

Moving my vegetables from one side of the plate to the

other, I couldn't help but think about Monica again. Where in the world was she? It wasn't like her not to be in touch. I made a mental note to give her a call tomorrow to make sure she was okay. Besides, I needed to confirm whether the bridal shop appointment would work for her too.

18 MONICA'S DRAMA

I dialed Monica's number, hearing the phone ring eight times before it rolled over to her voice mail.

"Hi Monica, this is Keisha. Where are you, girl? We've all been worried about you because it's just not like you to let weeks go by without calling or stopping by. Please give me a call as soon as you get this. Love you!"

Hopefully she would return my call before the end of the day, because if I didn't hear from her by this evening, Pam and I were going to stop by her place tomorrow after work. I called Jamel to see if he'd heard anything from Rico, but he hadn't spoken to him since the engagement party. He hadn't spoken to Monica either.

My cell phone rang just as I was ending the call to Jamel.

"Hello?"

"Hey, it's Pam. I just wanted to let you know that I heard the police were over at Monica's house this morning. I don't know what's going on over there, but they said PG County PD was all over the place. There were a couple of detectives there too with unmarked cars and everything, supposedly canvassing the neighborhood."

"Get out of here! Who told you that? What in the world do you think happened?"

"I don't know what happened, but you know Kimiko, the girl who does my hair? She lives right down the street from her and she said she saw all the cars over there when she was headed to the shop early this morning. I was getting ready to head over there. You want to come with me? I just don't want to go by myself, because I don't know what I might be rolling up on."

"I feel you. Can you swing by here to pick me up, or do you want me to come to your job?"

"I already left the office. I'm on my cell phone headed to you right now."

"Okay, I'll see you when you get here."

Meanwhile, I went into Tanya's office to let her know I was going to have to leave the office and might not be back for the rest of the day. She knew I was concerned about Monica and agreed to handle things around the office.

"If you need me to do anything, just call back here and I'll take care of it," Tanya offered while walking me to the door. "I pray to God she's okay."

"Me too. Thanks."

When we finally made it to Monica's house, there were still two police cars on the scene. One of the officers told us that Monica had been rushed to Med Star Southern Maryland Hospital due to an assault. We jumped back into the car and headed in the direction of the hospital after answering a couple of questions.

"What in the world could have happened to her?" asked Pam as she weaved in and out of traffic on Branch Avenue.

"I don't know, but I did know something was wrong. I told you, it wasn't like Monica to just not call."

At the hospital reception desk, we were told that Monica had been admitted and was in the ICU. Pam and I told the receptionist that we were her sisters and needed to see her immediately. Typically, family members were the only people they let into ICU to visit a patient. We were then referred to an area where a young doctor who looked to be about thirty years old met us in the visitor's waiting room.

"Hello, I'm Dr. Michaels."

"Hi, doctor. I'm Keisha and this is Pam. We're Monica's sisters. Can you please tell us what happened?"

"Well, the police received a 911 call from Monica's residence at about 7:30 this morning. The young lady on the phone, believed to be Monica told the 911 dispatcher that her boyfriend had attacked her. By the time the police arrived, she was unconscious on the floor and was bleeding from her nose and mouth. She has a very bad blow to the side of her head and a couple of bruises on her arms and back. I hate to be the one to have to tell you this, but she was also sexually assaulted."

"What? How could Rico do this to her?" Pam cried. "I mean, who rapes their own girlfriend?"

"There are two officers waiting across the hall in the second room on the right. They're hoping that you will be able to provide them with some information. A neighbor told the police that they saw a young man running through her front yard. The time the neighbor reported seeing someone matches up with the time of the 911 call."

"Thank you, Dr. Michaels. We'll talk to the officers now so we can get to the bottom of this."

"You're quite welcome. If there's anything that I can get for you, please let me know. Here's my card."

I handed the card to Pam and we headed across the hall as directed by Dr. Michaels. Both officers stood as we entered the room.

"Hello, we're Monica Stevens' sisters. I'm Keisha, and this is Pam."

"Hello ladies. We're the two detectives investigating the assault on your sister. I'm Detective Dixon and this is Detective Bines. We're trying to track down her boyfriend, because a neighbor believes that's who she saw running away from the house this morning."

"His name is Rico McDonald. He's a dancer over at that strip club in D.C. I can't remember the name of it, but he lives off Pennsylvania Avenue just across the D.C. line headed out of Maryland. I can't think of the name of the apartments, but I can show you where it is. Officer, exactly what happened?"

"Well, your sister called 911 this morning screaming that she was being beaten. Then the phone went dead. When officers arrived on the scene, her front door was open. While conducting a search of the premises, they found her lying in a pool of blood on her bedroom floor. She was unresponsive and still hasn't regained consciousness. We've been waiting here for her to wake up so we can talk to her."

Detective Bines left the room. I could hear him speaking with another detective on the phone. He was sending a car over to the club to look for Rico. Suddenly, I became very angry. Here was my girl lying in a hospital bed because he wanted to use her face as a punching bag. I couldn't wait to lay eyes on him. I needed to hear him tell me why he felt he could put his hands on her; and then to rape her? Who did he think he was? He would have to answer to this one way or another. Monica had too many friends and relatives who loved her. Some of them were even a little crazy. No one was going to let him get away with this.

Before heading in to see Monica, I called Darius to tell him what happened. He said he was going to call Jamel so he could call some of his people to see if anyone knew where Rico was. He'd have to be dealt with; and either the law was going to deal with him or street justice would take care of him. That's just the way it was.

19 POOR JUDGMENT

Pam and I stayed by Monica's bedside for the two days that she was in the ICU. On the third day, she was moved into a private room and had gained consciousness, although she couldn't recall many of the details of the attack; at least not immediately. The more we talked to her about it, the more I felt she was blocking it out to avoid replaying it in her mind. What she did say was unbelievable.

"A few days ago, I confronted him about my recent visit to the gynecologist for my checkup. I received a certified letter from the doctor's office informing me that I had an abnormal pap smear and needed to come in as soon as possible to talk to the doctor. When I arrived, I was informed that I had contracted a sexually transmitted disease. Chlamydia," she admitted. "So, I called Rico because he was the only person I'd had sex with. I didn't tell him over the phone because I wanted to talk to him in person.

"Monica, please tell me that you were not having unprotected sex with Rico. Girl, you had to know he was probably sleeping with more women than just you. I'm sorry.

I'm sure you really don't want to be lectured right now. Forgive me. Besides, I'm definitely not in a position to judge."

"I guess I was just being stupid by believing him when he told me that I was the only one. I really thought we had a future together. In hindsight, I really don't know what I was thinking," Monica wiped the tears from her right eye. "There were so many signs. I just chose to ignore them and look where it got me."

Looking closely at her face, I noticed no tears were flowing from her left eye, but she was extremely bruised and battered on that side of her face also. Her lip was busted, she had a black eye, and a huge laceration on the side of her head. Rico had really done a job on her. He attacked her like he was an animal.

"Monica, we just don't want to see you get caught out there. This situation could have gone a lot worse than it did. Thank God it's something you can get rid of and not something that could take you out of here," said Pam. Your injuries could have been a lot worse too. Rico could have killed you."

"Yeah, I know. They started me on the antibiotics early this morning. I just can't believe he put his hands on me like that. He just flipped out! When I told him what the doctor said, he stood there just looking at me for a good minute. The next thing I remember is him punching me in the eye. He forced me to have sex with him and then continued beating me until I felt like I was going to black out. I remember grabbing the phone and calling 911. He was pounding on my face while I was talking to the 911 operator. Then I passed out. You're right. He could have killed me," she tried not to cry again.

"I'm very pissed off right now. I really liked Rico and thought he was cool even though I didn't agree with his line of work. I try not to judge people. I just want to beat the life out of him right now," I admitted.

"It's okay. PG County Police picked him up last night. So, he's in jail."

"That's good news. Please let me know when you have to go to court so I can take off to go with you."

"Keisha, I want to thank you and Pam for being here for me through this."

"Girl, you know we wouldn't have had it any other way," Pam said, re-entering the room after grabbing some pretzels from the vending machine down the hall. "There's no need to thank us. This is what friends do. Oh, I mean sisters."

I went out to the nurse's station to find out what time Monica's dinner would be arriving. She was regaining her appetite and needed to keep her strength up. Pam and I decided Monica would be okay for the night. She needed to get some rest and we didn't want to be a distraction to her. I left her a book I'd bought at Barnes & Noble last weekend, but hadn't had a chance to read. If she felt up to it, at least she could read to keep busy. Shawn called to tell Monica that she might not make it to the hospital because Tyrone was out of town and wouldn't be able to watch the kids.

I called Darius while driving home from the hospital that evening to tell him that Rico had been arrested. He was relieved to hear the news.

"Baby, I know you're probably tired because of the busy schedule over the past couple of days. Trying to go to work and spend the evenings at the hospital had to be challenging for you. Have you been feeling okay? You're always so busy with everyone else that you rarely focus on your own health."

"Thanks for thinking of me. Now that I know Monica's going to be okay. I'm okay. Regarding my health; I haven't been having too many issues lately except some achy joints. You know, that's normal anyway."

"That's good to know. You know I worry about that. Just come on home. Dinner should be ready by the time you get here."

"Baby, you didn't have to do that. Yes, I did. I love you and I wanted to make sure you had a home-cooked meal. If you've been eating at that hospital, I'm probably going to have to admit you in a day or so anyway."

"You're silly. I should be home in about twenty minutes, okay?"

"That's fine, babe. Just drive safely and I'll see you when you get here."

"I love you."

"I love you too."

I was so blessed to have such an amazing man in my life. I just couldn't express it enough, and I'm certain people were probably getting tired of hearing it but, oh well. I never worried about him cheating, he never put his hands on me and we hardly ever disagreed about anything, but when we did it was peaceful and we always resolved it before going to bed. Then, we would make love like nothing ever happened. Makeup sex was the best. I loved him so much and rejoiced all the way home about where we were in our lives at this moment. I couldn't wait to be his wife.

20 LET'S DO THIS RIGHT!

Darius made linguini with clams in a white clam sauce and salad for dinner. He was a pretty good cook, and took every meal he ever made for me very seriously.

"Babe, this is delicious!"

"You know you're my baby, and that means only the best for you."

"So, Monica's gonna be okay?"

"Yes, she'll be fine. She just made a big mistake by getting involved with Rico. I knew he was going to bring her heartache, but you know I was trying to stay out of her affairs. So, I didn't say anything negative about their relationship. I don't know, I've just had a bad feeling about him since I met him."

"It's probably a good thing you didn't get involved. She may have resented you for it if you had. Knowing Monica, you would have said something to piss her off and the two of you would have fallen out. You would have been mad at yourself if your friendship ended because of something you said to her too. You know it. Monica was going to have to see who Rico really was for herself, and it looks like that's what happened. Now, you all are gonna have to help her get over him so she can move on with her life."

"You're right about that. I don't even want to think about that right now, as long as I know she's going to be okay; I feel better already about it. Enough about Monica and Rico. I wanna talk about you, Big Daddy." I pulled him so close to me, I could feel the pound of his heart through his sweater.

"Girl, don't you start nothing you can't finish. The old me would take you upstairs right now and handle things, but the respectful Darius is trying to hold back. So, you better cut it out, babe."

"Yeah, okay. I hear you. Better learn how to fight the temptation."

He led me upstairs to the bedroom where candles lined the dresser and night stand. He picked up the remote to the TV and put on one of the R & B music channels. An old Kem song played softly in the background. I stood in front of him wearing nothing but a pair of black panties. I climbed onto the bed and waited for Darius to join me. I loved watching him remove his clothes. He was so sexy in his nakedness that I immediately became aroused. So did he.

"Why don't you lay down?" I asked.

I climbed on top of him, but he wouldn't look at me.

"Keisha, you better stop."

"What? Really?"

"Yes, I wasn't playing when I told you that I was trying to live better. Don't tempt me. Besides, didn't you just tell me that I better learn how to fight the temptation?"

"Yes, I did say that," sighing as I rested on the bed next to him. You're really serious about this, aren't you?"

"Yes, I'm serious. I didn't realize you were such a temptress, though," he laughed.

"I didn't realize you were serious."

"Keisha, I meant what I said about love and respect. I should have respected you like this the first time around, but I didn't. It looks like I actually created a monster if you ask me."

"Well, nobody asked you,"

"What? Let me find out you've got a little attitude because you can't get what you want. I feel so used," he joked.

"I'm glad you find all of this so amusing."

"No, all jokes aside. As much as I want to partake in every inch of you, I really want to know that I can hold out. At least let me try, please? I promise you, if you ride with me on this; you won't be sorry in the end. Imagine what our wedding night will be like if we stop having sex now and wait. Granted, we've already messed up by doing it in the first place; but we don't have to keep doing it."

"Darius, you know what? You're right. I'm sorry I've been putting so much pressure on you about it. I know better. I used to be a good girl and never did things like this when I was faithfully going to church and Bible study. I know that I have to stay close to God, or I can be a very bad girl."

"The truth is, we could both improve by staying closer to God. Think about me and what I've been through. Yes, I go to AA meetings and all, but with God things could be so much better. I really believe it. So, until we say I do in front of God and our families and loved ones, we're going to have to do our very best to keep from slipping up again."

"Wow, babe. I'm proud of you. Where was this Darius when we first met? I wouldn't have had to worry about being tempted if this guy was the one I met at the Food Lion."

"He didn't really exist back then, but he's here now. I told you I was going to make an honest woman out of you. I want to make an honest man out of myself too, so let's do this. Where are my pajamas? I suggest you put some on too."

Darius was right. We really needed to do what we could to live right. The truth is, the passion between us was so amazing that it could sustain us through not only the night, but an entire lifetime. I truly believed we shared a love that few people ever got to experience. It was the greatest romance, and we were living it one day at a time. Even without the sex. I pulled my flannel pajamas out of the drawer and put them on. This was going to be very interesting.

21 THAT'S WHAT FRIENDS ARE FOR

I turned the key in the door lock to Monica's condo before Darius and I escorted her in. She was still a little stiff and was moving very slowly. The truth is, I believed she was in more pain than she let on because she knew I would worry. Darius supported her waist with his arm to steady her steps as she crossed the threshold. The living room was still in disarray because there hadn't been anyone to clean up the mess while Monica was in the hospital. I wished I'd had more time. The last thing I wanted was for her to come home to the reminder of what happened that day.

"Are you okay?" I looked directly into Monica's eyes, knowing her expression would reveal the answer.

"I'm just glad you two are here."

"Well, there was no way we were going to let you come in here alone. I'm sorry that I didn't get this place cleaned up before we brought you home. I had no idea how bad it really was."

Darius sat down on the sofa. Holding his head in his hands, he began to tap one foot on the floor.

"Rico is gonna get messed up! What could have gotten into him to make him do something like this? Look at this place! He not only did a number on her, but this place is a wreck! He has to pay!"

"Baby, let the law handle him. He's in jail and he'll have his day in court. Don't even think about doing anything crazy. Do you hear me? You've got way too much to lose, and that person doesn't even exist anymore, remember? You're a different person now. Didn't we just talk about this last night?"

"Darius, please listen to Keisha. It's not worth it! You've got too many good things going on right now to mess it up because of him!" Monica cried, taking a seat on the sofa next to him. "I don't want to see anything happen to you because of him.

"Let me get your bed ready."

I entered Monica's bedroom and the reality of that morning hit me like an 18-wheeler. The lamp rested on the floor next to the bed. The curtains had been pulled halfway off the rod and were hanging on the floor. The phone jack had been ripped from the wall and the receiver was off its base. It had come to rest on the bathroom floor. There were still blood stains on the carpet and specks of blood lining the wall and floorboard alongside Monica's bed. She must have been scared out of her mind!

This looked like a scene from the First 48. I loved watching the show on A &E on Thursday evenings. Shawn often accused me of being crazy because the show is very gruesome. It's a reality based detective show that maps out the first 48 hours of cases that almost always resulted in at least one homicide. Thank God Rico didn't kill her. That whole ordeal could have gone a lot worse than it did. Monica was still here. She could testify against him in court. There were a lot of victims of crimes just like this that never got that opportunity because they had been silenced.

I began picking up things that were scattered all over the floor. Pulling a fresh set of sheets from her linen closet, I made her bed so that it was nice and fresh. The dirty fitted sheet was missing. Probably taken as evidence. After everything was back in its original place, I vacuumed the floor. The specks of blood were gone from the walls, although there was a blood stain the size of an iPad on the carpet that I couldn't fully remove. Darius and I relocated an accent rug she had in another area of the room. We wanted to cover it up so she wouldn't have to look at it, at least until a professional carpet cleaner could do some work on it. Before going into the living room to get Monica, I gave the room another once over.

"Monica, I straightened out the room for you and put fresh sheets on your bed. You want to take a shower while Darius and I wait out here?"

"Yeah, if you don't mind I would like to do that. I really appreciate everything you guys have done. I love you guys." Tears rolled down her cheeks as she took short slow steps toward the bedroom. "Darius, thanks for being here too."

I turned on the shower, pulled fresh pajamas and panties from her lingerie drawer and placed them on the vanity in the bathroom.

"You go ahead. We'll be in the living room when you get out. If you need me, yell and I'll be right there."

"I know you will." Touching my cheek, I was hoping she didn't feel the moisture from the tears I'd wiped away when she wasn't looking.

Darius and I began cleaning the living room while she was in the shower. The glass tea light holder that looked like a mini lamp I'd bought her at Pier One just a few weeks ago was in pieces all over the floor. The glass in the painting that hung on the wall behind the sofa was broken and scattered all over the place.

"I remember when she bought this painting. It's called Forever My Lady. That girl sacrificed food to buy this. She bought it right after college graduation as a way of celebrating her accomplishment. The artist actually did a show at Hampton University while we were there."

"She told me that story a while back. I'll take it over to the framing shop to have the glass replaced tomorrow," Darius placed the painting next to the front door so he wouldn't forget to grab it on our way out.

"I'm sure she would appreciate that. You're the best, babe. "

I headed toward Monica's bedroom when I heard her turn off the shower. Knocking on the bathroom door, I waited for her response.

"I'll be out in a second!" She yelled from the other side.

"I just wanted to make sure you were okay. You want me to make you a bowl of soup or something?"

"That would be great! Thanks!"

Darius had already pulled a container of Cream of Potato soup from the refrigerator and was searching for a pot when I entered the kitchen.

"Babe, they're in the cabinet next to the stove."

"Thanks, Love. Is she okay?"

"She's fine. I'm just glad that we could be here for her.

I grabbed the broom and began cleaning up the broken glass.

"Jamel said he was coming over to sit with her for a few hours. He should be here in a little while."

After warming up the soup, Darius poured it into a bowl. He placed several Toll House crackers on a napkin on the tray. He poured ginger ale into a glass filled with ice. After he was done, I took the tray into Monica's bedroom and placed it on the nightstand.

"You didn't have to do all of that."

"I didn't. Darius did."

"Thank you, Darius!" She yelled from the bedroom.

"You're welcome!" He headed to the door to let Jamel in.

"Hey Man!"

"Hey, Darius. Where's my girl?" Jamel asked, heading down the hall to Monica's bedroom.

"Hey, baby!" She said reaching toward him for a hug.

"How are you feeling?" He asked, brushing her hair back with his hand.

"I'm okay. I'm so glad you came over."

"You know you're my boo. How could I not come?"

Darius came into the room and took a seat on the chaise in front of the window while Jamel took a seat on the bed next to her.

"Well, ya'll can go now. I'm here and I'll make sure that she's okay."

"Well, dang! Why does it sound like you're trying to get rid of us?"

"No, it's not like that. I know you've been with her since the incident happened. Let me do my part now. You're being relieved."

"Thanks, I think."

Darius kissed Monica on her cheek before helping me put on my coat. He headed toward the living room while I said good-bye.

"Girl, if you need me you know where I am."

"I know. Thanks for everything."

Darius and I walked to the car hand in hand. I took my seat on the passenger side after he opened the door. After placing Monica's artwork in the trunk of his car, he got into the driver's seat.

Lord, please take care of Monica. Help her to make

smarter decisions from here on out. In fact, we could all stand to make some changes in our lives, but for right now; I want to thank you for sparing her life. Please let her experience be a testimony to other women in similar relationships. No one deserves to be abused like that. Amen.

"Are you okay?" Darius asked after putting his seatbelt on. He wiped away the tears that were flowing down my face.

"Yes, I'm fine. I was just talking to God. He's going to fix this. I know He is."

22 RICO'S DAY IN COURT

We were seated in court for about thirty minutes before the judge came in. Monica, Pam, Shawn, Jamel, Darius and I took up an entire row. Several of her family members had shown up as well. Cynthia Parker was also in the courtroom, but none of us knew what she looked like. The Washington Post article didn't include a picture.

Rico, wearing a jailhouse jumpsuit, shackled at the feet and waist glanced in our direction before taking his seat. Unlike the man we thought we knew, he looked like a monster. Someone with no heart or feelings was standing before us. Someone who could physically abuse and sexually assault not one, but two women was standing there looking like a hard-core criminal. I suppose he was, after all of this.

"Can you believe him? He has the nerve to look over here after what he did to you!" Shawn whispered to Monica, shaking her head in disgust. "I wish I could slap the taste out of his mouth! Knock that stupid look right off his face!"

Rico had been charged with assault just weeks after he attacked Monica. An article ran in the Washington Post regarding a woman who had been beaten and bound before being thrown into a closet for three days straight with no food or water when she tried to end her relationship with him. Rico had caught a flight to Atlanta, leaving her there bound and gagged. She fought to free herself from the ropes and on the third day, she escaped; banging on doors of nearby apartments until someone would let her in.

An elderly woman who lived at the end of the hall answered and called the police. The woman, 34-year-old Cynthia Parker was taken to the hospital for overnight observation, which turned into four days. There was a warrant for Rico's arrest. The article said someone had called the crime stoppers hotline to say that he was scheduled to fly back on a flight arriving at Regan National Airport. Once the plane landed, Rico was arrested and held without bond. If his lawyer hadn't petitioned the court for bail in Monica's case, the second incident might not have happened. She was also raped. The system had already failed both women by allowing him to roam the streets instead of remaining in jail until court.

Rico and his attorney stood after the case was called.

"Mr. McDonald, you're being charged with two counts of domestic assault and battery, two counts of aggravated assault, two counts of sexual assault and one count of unlawful imprisonment. How do you plead to each of these charges?" the judge asked.

"Not guilty, your Honor."

"There were gasps throughout the courtroom from Monica's sister and brother. Her mother, who was sitting next to her, began weeping.

"Mom, it's okay," said Monica, rubbing her mother's shoulder.

"All right, Mr. McDonald. This case will begin on February 20, 2017 at 9:00 AM." The judge made eye contact with the attorney.

"Do you have any questions, Mr. McDonald?"

"No, Sir."

As quickly as the judge called the case, he was on to the next one. It was unbelievable how many people were waiting to go before the judge. There were women sitting all over the courtroom and very few men at all. This was an indication that domestic violence cases were consuming the judge's docket today. Probably every day.

He had some nerve pleading not guilty when he knows what he did to her. This was going to be an open and shut case considering he had not only attacked Monica, but had sexually assaulted the other woman and held her against her will. Thank God, both women were alive to testify against him. Sadly, what happened to Monica almost couldn't even be compared to what happened to Cynthia.

As we headed out of the courthouse, a young woman approached Monica.

"Excuse me, Monica?" she inquired.

"Yes, may I help you?"

"My name is Cynthia Parker. I'm the woman Rico attacked after you."

"Oh, my God. I am so sorry!"

"Don't be sorry. It wasn't your fault. I didn't realize I was dealing with such a psychotic person until it was too late. I just wanted to introduce myself to you because I understand what you're going through. I've been through the same hell as you. I wanted to let you know that I stand in support of you and what happened that day."

"I'm happy to meet you. Are you okay?" Monica asked sincerely.

"I'm getting there."

"Do you mind if I ask you exactly what happened?"

"Rico and I have been . . . had been seeing each other for about six months. He had told me that you were his ex-girlfriend, which is how I knew your name. Rico was constantly disappearing on me, so I knew something was up with him; I just couldn't put my finger on it. Monica, I didn't even know that he was a dancer until he was arrested and the article ran in the paper. He told me he was a lab technician at the hospital. Anyway, I was getting fed up with him and his cheating ways, so I told him that I no longer wanted to see him," she paused, staring into space as if she were playing the events back in her mind.

"He threatened me when I tried to leave. He told me that my parents would find my body floating in the Potomac River if I left him. He said he would tell them that I went shopping and never returned. He threatened to slash my face up with a knife, holding it to my cheek. I tried to run, but he grabbed me and threw me down on the bed. He started ripping off my clothes and then he raped me," Cynthia sobbed. "After he was finished, he started punching me in the face as I cried uncontrollably on the bed. He tied my feet together while I fought to break free. I couldn't get away. I was punching him and scratching at his face, but he was stronger. He tied my hands and threw me into the closet. I remember trying to scream for help, but no one could hear me; especially with the tape over my mouth. I prayed to God for help. I asked him to save me, and the next thing I remember is waking up three days later fighting for my life. I got out of the ropes and ran like hell."

"God answered your prayers," Monica told her as they hugged.

"Now, we have to make sure that he gets convicted and doesn't get released for a very long time. Do you mind if I ask you a personal question?" Monica waited for permission to continue.

"You can ask me anything."

"I know this is gonna sound like a strange question, but

did he use a condom when he raped you?"

"No, he didn't. I already know though," she admitted. "After the attack, they ran some tests at the hospital. That's when I found out I had contracted a STD. Unfortunately, Rico and I had slept together numerous times without protection anyway. So, I may have contracted it prior to the rape and just didn't know I had it."

"That was the reason why he attacked me. I confronted him about giving me a disease and he lost it," Monica admitted. Jamel and Darius looked at each other very strangely because neither of them knew what had caused Rico to snap that day. I hadn't mentioned it to either one of them because it wasn't my news to tell.

"Well, I'm sorry about what happened to you. I'm sorry that either of us had to go through this, but we have to remain strong. I'll be in court every day during the trial."

"Monica, so will I. Please take my numbers just in case you need something or just want to talk." Cynthia handed her a card with her work and cell phone numbers on it.

"Here are my numbers too. If you need me, just call. I mean that," Monica handed her a card also.

In her mind, she wanted to hurt him for what he did to her. Prayerfully, justice would have its way and he would go away for a very long time. Society didn't need men like Rico running around raping and beating women, not to mention spreading diseases around. While, both women should have taken precautions to prevent themselves from catching anything if they were going to sleep with him, he should have protected them. He knew he was sleeping around with multiple women even if they didn't know. This would surely be a wakeup call for Monica if I knew her the way I thought I did. Hopefully, it would be one for Cynthia too. She seemed like a very nice woman and just like Monica, she didn't deserve what she got.

TERRI SEYMORE-GREEN

23 THE WRONG MAN

While driving to my office that morning, I couldn't help but wonder how many other women Rico might have been seeing. Both Monica and Cynthia believed they were in exclusive relationships with him. He was pretty slick to have gotten away with it for as long as he did without getting caught. I just kept thinking how much worse it could have been. I remembered the conversation Shawn, Pam, and I had over lunch right before this happened. We talked about Rico having a side chick. If he'd been dating Cynthia for as long as she said, Monica was actually the side chick. I still couldn't believe this happened.

Monica would have to start using better judgment when it came to men. Throughout college, she slept with this one and that one. Monica was always the life of the party and was known for dating a football player or fraternity brother. She just liked those types of guys. Not that all athletes or frat brothers were bad, but she surely knew how to pick them.

They were always the ones who dogged her by flaunting other women right in front of her face. She never said a word and just took whatever they dished out. Once, she'd even caught her boyfriend about to have sex with another woman. She had visited his dorm late one evening. As she approached the door, she could hear noises coming from the room. When she turned the door knob, it opened and there he was with a girl from her Anthropology class down on her knees about to do God only knows what with him. They were both completely naked, so one can only imagine what was about to happen next or what might have already happened. Monica ran from the room crying and I thought she would be done with him after she explained what happened. The next day, I spotted the two of them over at the Student Union having lunch. I never understood it because she's a beautiful person both inside and out. Could her self-esteem be suffering so much that she stood for anything? We would need to work on that.

Cynthia was also educated, holding down a high paying government job, she was beautiful, owned her own home, and seemed to have everything going for her. How in the world did she end up with Rico? Either one of them could have had their pick of a lot of handsome, eligible bachelor's in the DC area that would have treated them with the love and respect they deserved, but neither of them commanded it. They both just needed to learn how to make better decisions when it came to the men they let into their lives.

They were blessed to have God watching over them. Both could have been killed at the hands of Rico. They could have been infected with something much worse than Chlamydia. I prayed that this would be a lesson learned for them both. At least they had each other to get through this. They were two women who were guilty of one thing; loving the wrong man.

24 THE NEWS

(Three Months Later). I called Tanya on her cell phone early enough to open the office for me.

"Girl, I really appreciate you going in on your day off. I feel horrible and believe I just need some rest. My stomach is turning faster than the spin cycle on my Samsung washing machine. I'd better go. I feel it coming on again," I ran into the bathroom.

"Keisha, please take care of yourself. I've got it. If you need anything else, please let me know."

The truth is, I hadn't been feeling that great for several days. Throwing up seemed to be the only thing that eased the feeling inside of me, at least for the moment. It had been four days, and I couldn't manage to keep much down, although last night, a small cup of chicken noodle soup stayed with me about as long as watered down perfume. Today was the first day that I'd thrown up multiple times, so I knew it was time to do something about it. For months, I had been taking folic acid and extra iron to help replenish my red blood cells under my doctor's orders. She recently pulled me off both supplements, so I thought perhaps this was my body's way of going through some sort of withdrawal. For that reason only, I dismissed my illness as being nothing serious and went back to sleep. I made a note to call the doctor as soon as I woke up. My body wouldn't be able to take this much longer.

Around 10:30, rays from the sun crept through my miniblinds and onto my face. On any other morning, I would have embraced it as a blessing that God had allowed me to have another day. Today, it reminded me of an annoying little brother or sister determined to disturb their big sister's beauty sleep, and she couldn't understand why her parents bought a two-bedroom house when they knew they intended on expanding the family. I was very annoyed, but took it as a sign to get my butt out of bed and call the doctor. I also embraced the thought that I didn't have any annoying little brothers or sisters growing up.

"Good morning, Doctor Cavanaugh's office," said the receptionist in her usual perky voice.

I'd heard it many times before and it didn't bother me, but today was different. My patience was short because I just didn't feel good, but I tried to sound half as excited as she did just because it was the right thing to do. She either drank way too much coffee, or things were so fabulous in her life that she insisted on spreading her fabulousness around so that everyone could have some.

"Hello, this is Keisha Johnston calling. I was wondering if Doctor Cavanaugh had any openings for this afternoon."

"Hi Miss Johnston, let me look at her schedule. Would you mind holding for a moment?"

Running into the bathroom with the cordless phone, I hugged the toilet again. This time, I just stayed on the floor. For one, because I still felt nauseous and knew another episode would soon follow, and two, I didn't have the energy to get up. I was weak from the lack of nourishment and my stomach muscles were sore from the dry heaves. Today was turning out to be a not-so-good day if you asked me, so I prayed that nobody would. Dr. Cavanaugh was probably going to have to put me back on the supplements if this was a consequence of not taking them. Plus, I had to go to work tomorrow. I never liked being out more than a day unless I was hospitalized, which had happened a couple of times in recent years.

"Miss Johnston? You're in luck. Doctor Cavanaugh had a 2:00 o'clock cancellation. Will that work for you?"

"Yes, 2 PM is perfect."

"What is the visit for?"

"I haven't been able to keep anything on my stomach for several days now. I just haven't been feeling well. Maybe the flu or something. I'm not sure."

"Well, we'll let Doctor Cavanaugh get to the bottom of it. That's why she gets paid the big bucks," the receptionist laughed almost uncontrollably at what she thought was a joke. It wasn't funny. At least not today.

"Thank you, I'll see you at 2:00."

"You're very welcome!"

I stepped into the shower and embraced the warm water like I hadn't showered all week. The continuous vomiting made me feel dirty and I needed to rid myself of that feeling. Fortunately, Darius went to work early. There was no way I wanted him to see me this way because he worried about my health so much. I hadn't had a Sickle Cell Crisis in quite a while, praise the Lord; but the last time I did, I thought he was going to have a meltdown.

It was a hot day in May. For three days prior, I was having severe joint pain and knew that it was a bad sign. The thing about me is that I have a high tolerance for pain, so I tried to press through. By the evening of the third day, I couldn't even stand from a sitting position and I was running an extremely high fever. Darius called 911, but it seemed like it was taking forever for them to get there, so he picked me up and carried me to his car. We were at the hospital in ten minutes.

Prayerfully, I was not seriously ill because he was the last person I wanted to have to tell. Things were going so great in our lives that we didn't need any bad news. No flu, no Sickle Cell Crisis; not even an ingrown toenail. I just wanted to remain on the same path to happily ever after we'd been on since getting back together.

After I was dressed, I decided I better try to eat something. I sliced a bagel in half and popped it into the toaster. A little light cream cheese on half of it would be plenty to hold my stomach. Besides, I didn't want to fill up just in case I felt nauseous again. I drank a glass of cranberry juice to wash it down. Just as I was putting my plate and glass into the dishwasher, the phone rang.

"Hello?"

"Hey baby cakes! Are you okay? I called the office and Tanya said you weren't coming in."

"Hey babe. I haven't been feeling well. I didn't want to worry you, but I've been feeling sick to my stomach. Dr. Cavanaugh is going to see me at 2:00 o'clock today. I'm thinking it's those two supplements that I was taking and then had to suddenly stop. My body might be trying to tell me something," I said in a tone I hoped would convince him that I was okay.

"Do you need me to head that way so that I can go with you?"

"No, I'm fine. If I thought it was something serious, I would say yes. I've got it under control. Besides, aren't you supposed to managing air traffic or something?"

"Yes, but I can get one of the guys to cover for me for a

couple of hours if you need me."

"Darius, I really appreciate that but I'm okay. If something changes, I'll definitely call you."

"Please call me after the appointment, okay?"

"You'll be the first person I call. I promise."

I really didn't want to interrupt his day. Since his promotion to management, I tried not to call or visit too much. His career was on the rise, which meant a better life for both of us. So, I kept a lot of things to myself until he came home at night.

I arrived at Dr. Cavanaugh's office twenty minutes prior to my appointment. The nurse checked me in early so that she could get my vitals before the doctor came in.

"Your blood pressure's fine and your temperature is normal," the nurse said. "How has your appetite been?"

"My appetite has been normal. I haven't been eating any more or any less than usual, but I just can't keep much down. I'm not sure what's going on. I haven't added anything new to my diet, but I eat and within a few minutes or so, I'm heading to the bathroom."

"Well, Dr. Cavanaugh will be with you in a couple of minutes. Here's a gown for you to put on. If you need anything before she comes in, just hit this buzzer and I'll be right here."

"Thank you."

I changed into the traditional ugly hospital gown and tied it in the back. I could never remember whether it was supposed to be tied in the front or the back, so by default, I always tied it in the back. The nurse always told me, but everything usually became a blur very quickly because I hated doctor's visits. When you live with a serious illness, those visits can be a little overwhelming, so everything out of the nurse's mouth from the time that she handed me the gown sounded like Charlie Brown's school teacher from the

Peanuts cartoons.

Dr. Cavanaugh knocked on the door before entering.

"Hi, Keisha. How are you today?"

"I'm not feeling too well."

"What's been going on?"

"Well, a few days ago, I started feeling nauseous. I haven't been able to keep much of anything on my stomach. I threw up last night and again twice this morning. Days prior to that, I was just nauseous; but now I'm throwing up everything."

"Have you eaten today?"

"I had half a bagel with cream cheese and a glass of cranberry juice a couple of hours ago, because my stomach was empty from throwing up so much."

"Well, the first thing that I would like to do is run some blood work. I want to take a look at your cells to make sure that everything is okay in that area. Secondly, I would like you to take a pregnancy test."

"Huh?"

"Well, the nausea is a concern for me. When was your last period?"

"It was several weeks ago, I think; but you know I don't have regular periods. Remember? They're always early or late at least a week every month."

"I know, but we'd better be safe. We can get to the answer through the process of elimination. We'll start with the easy things first."

"Okay, but I assure you I am not pregnant, at least I don't think. My fiancé and I have been very careful for the most part."

"It's for the most part that concerns me," Dr. Cavanaugh smiled before exiting the room.

The lab technician came in pushing a cart filled with syringes, tubes, gauze, band-aids, and a few other items.

Some of them I knew she wouldn't be using on me. Within a few minutes, multiple tubes with colorful tops were filled with samples that would hopefully reveal what was going on.

"Ms. Johnston, I need to get a urine sample," she handed me the clear plastic cup with the screw-on top.

"Once you're done, please leave the sample in the little window in the bathroom and come back here to wait for Dr. Cavanaugh."

"Thanks," I said as I gathered the back of the gown and headed toward the bathroom.

After emptying my bladder and filling the cup with a generous sample, I headed back to the room as directed. I became anxious while waiting. I just wanted things to get back to normal. I wouldn't be able to enjoy any of Darius's home cooked meals or anything as long as I was feeling like this. Getting lost in my thoughts, I closed my eyes and fell asleep until there was a light tap on the door.

"Keisha, it looks like we were able to find out why you've been feeling so under the weather lately."

"Well, what is it?"

"Well, it's as I suspected. You're pregnant."

"What?"

"We tested both your urine and blood. Both tests came back positive. You're pregnant."

I sat on the examining room table with my mouth wide open, not knowing what to say. *How in the world would I tell Darius that I was pregnant? What about our wedding? Would he want to do it sooner or wait until after the baby was born? Would he even want me to keep it? Maybe he'd think I did it on purpose. What in the world was I going to do? Oh, my God! A baby!*

"You take a few days to let this sink in. We'll need to get you back in to see the OB-GYN for a vaginal exam so we can determine how far you are. Considering you had a period last month, you shouldn't be that far. So, are congratulations in order?"

"Yes, I suppose so," I wasn't sure, but it sounded like the right thing to say, considering.

"Okay, I'll see you very soon. Keisha, considering your Sickle Cell history, we really need to get you started with your prenatal care as soon as possible. The OB-GYN will want to see you more often than someone without your health concerns. You do understand that, right?"

"Yes, I do. Dr. Cavanaugh, do you really think that I can pull this off?"

"Absolutely! With proper care, we'll be delivering a beautiful, strong, healthy baby in no time."

"That's very important to me. A healthy and strong baby. Wow, I can't believe this. A baby!"

"Congratulations, again."

"Yes! Thanks, Dr. Cavanaugh. I'm not sure how my fiancé is going to take this news, but it's definitely a blessing."

Driving down Branch Avenue, all I could think about was how I would break the news to Darius. I couldn't believe it, I was pregnant. It wasn't the way I had planned it, but God didn't make mistakes. My mom always said that. Life had changed so much in such a short time, but I was excited about sharing a child with Darius. We were going to have our family a lot sooner than I thought. I couldn't stop smiling. I remembered my promise to call him after my appointment, but this wasn't news suitable for a phone call. We would talk when he came home. I hoped I could get myself together enough to make him a good meal. With this type news, I better plan on making dessert too.

25 GOD KEEPS ON BLESSING

My euphoric state made the drive back home seem effortless despite the traffic. I can't say I even remembered crossing an intersection, stopping at a red light, a stop sign or anything else. I just remembered pulling into my garage where I sat in my car wondering how I would break the news to Darius. Would he be as happy as I hoped he would, or would he be disappointed in me; disappointed in us? Darius Jr. was almost fourteen years old now and Darius had spoken in the past of having a daughter someday.

This wasn't how I planned it, but some things we had no control over. Well we did have control over it; but that went out the window with all the good love making that had been going on when we first got back together. I mean, we started out strong by using protection until the second episode that night. Lately, we hadn't been doing anything at all. I guess we both got caught up in the amazing feeling of my skin against his, and now look. The plan to wait to have a baby a year or two into the marriage was done. The important thing right now was figuring out the best way to tell him.

I picked up the phone and dialed Pam's cell phone

number instead, hoping she would have some advice about how to tell the love of my life that we were having a little one. Pam could also keep secrets, so I knew I didn't have to worry about the word getting out before I was ready. Shawn on the other hand would have it on tonight's 6:00 o'clock news.

"Hey girl, what's up?" she said without ever saying hello.

"Hey."

"What's wrong with you?"

"You are not going to believe this."

"What? What's wrong?"

"Pam, I went to the doctor this morning because I haven't been feeling well. I found out I'm pregnant."

"What? Why you playing?"

"No, I'm serious. Remember how I was throwing up the other day? It's been going on ever since, so this afternoon I went to the doctor. Now, I know why I've been so sick. There's an embryo in there cutting up. I'm pregnant!"

"What did Darius have to say?"

"I haven't told him yet. You're the first person I've told and you're being sworn to secrecy right now!"

"You know you can trust me. Promise me one thing, though."

"What?"

"The minute you tell him, you better call me back!"

"Okay. I was hoping you might have an idea for a clever way to break the news."

Pam immediately laid out a plan that she thought would work. She was fast on her feet when it came to things like this.

"Congratulations! Y'all are gonna have a pretty little baby! I get to be a part of the auntie team! I am so excited!"

"We have to get through a wedding first. This is probably going to change things a little. I'll let you know."

"Well, whatever you two decide to do; you know I'm right there with you. I love you, girl."

"I love you too. Thanks."

Darius would be getting off in about an hour. I pulled some salmon from the freezer and defrosted it in the microwave. Salmon, rice pilaf and broccoli, cauliflower and carrots would make a healthy dinner. I would have to tell him tonight so we could start thinking about our next move. I was praying that he wouldn't want to keep the scheduled wedding date of next June. At the same time, I didn't want him to marry me just because I was pregnant, either. What if he wanted me to get an abortion? That was out of the question. I mean, we weren't planning on having a baby this soon, but we would have to figure it all out. So many thoughts raced through my head almost as fast as my race to the bathroom. Here we go again.

I had to make a run to the store before starting dinner if I was going to go with Pam's suggested plan. After arriving back at the house, I raced around the kitchen trying to get the salmon seasoned and in the oven. I washed the vegetables, cut them up and steamed them while the rice pilaf simmered on the stove. I practiced my announcement a few times, then I waited.

"Hey Honey." He kissed my lips and held me close to him. "How are you feeling?"

"I'm fine. Thanks for asking." I pulled two plates and glasses from the cabinet and placed them on the table. After removing silverware for two from the drawer, I placed those on the table also. I felt beads of sweat starting to build up on my forehead. Darius came over to the table to help.

"Babe, what in the world is wrong with you? You're sweating like crazy! I couldn't even make you do that when we used to make love long and hard! What's up?" Darius laughed, and grabbed me around the waist to pull me closer to him.

"Dinner's ready. Let me make the plates and I'll be right back." Walking back into the kitchen, I dodged the question.

"Keisha, what's wrong baby?"

"Nothing's wrong. I'll be right back. Wash your hands and have a seat, please."

I fixed our plates and placed them on the table. Darius joined me after a minute. Reaching for my hands, he blessed the food.

"Lord, thank you for this delicious meal that my baby has prepared. Please make it nourishing to our bodies. Thank you for blessing us with the love that will carry us through until the end of our time and beyond. Amen."

"Amen."

"Everything looks delicious. I wasn't expecting dinner tonight. I was thinking we were probably going to go out to grab something. You sure surprised me. So, what did Dr. Cavanaugh have to say today?"

"Well, she wanted to run some blood work to check my cells. Babe, here. I baked some rolls."

"How did that go? He reached into the bread basket to pull out a roll."

"My cells are fine."

"Well, do you have some sort of virus or something? I heard there's something going around. I've been trying not to catch it, but it looks like it got you. Wait a minute."

Darius pulled the pacifier that was hidden under the rolls from the bread basket.

"Babe, what in the world?" He looked from the pacifier to me quizzically.

"Baby, I don't have a virus."

"Wait a minute! Are you trying to tell me we're having a baby?" He stood.

"Darius, yes. I'm pregnant."

155

Staring at me, he took a sip of his iced tea. Swallowing deeply, he stared again with an expressionless look on his face, then a grin.

"Say something."

"Whoo-hoo! My baby's having my baby!" He yelled. "Keisha, if this is your idea of a joke, it's not funny. So, if it is, please come clean now while you still can."

"Darius, I'm serious. Dr. Cavanaugh did the blood test and a urine test; both came back positive."

"Yes, baby!" Grabbing me around the waist, he picked me up. Spinning me around and around in his arms.

"Darius, please stop before I throw up again."

"Oh, baby. I forgot. We're having a baby! I've got to call somebody. Anybody!"

He picked up the phone and dialed his parents' phone number. After the third ring, Candice answered.

"Hello?"

"Ma, guess what? Keisha and I just found out something today."

"She's pregnant!"

"How'd you know?"

"I didn't, but you're way to excited to be telling me you got a new puppy," Candice laughed. "Congratulations, son! Let me speak to her."

"Hi, Mom."

"Hey, baby. So, I'm going to be a grandma again, huh?"

"Yes, you are. It's definitely not how we expected it to happen, but I got the results today."

"So, have you guys decided to change the wedding date? I mean, don't let me put pressure on you but it would be nice if my grandbaby could come into this world with two loving parents who are married. You know what I mean?"

"Yes, I know. Darius and I haven't had the chance to discuss any of that yet. I just broke the news to him and he immediately called you."

"That's my boy. Well, whatever you two decide to do, you know I'm there for you. John's not home right now, but I'll be sure to pass the news on to him when he gets here. I sure would love to have a granddaughter. You know I'll be happy with whatever God blesses us with as long as the baby's healthy; but a granddaughter would be wonderful!"

"I know, Mom. Once I go to see the OB-GYN, I'll let you know when the due date will be. Meantime, we need to talk about some things; so, I better get going. I'll keep you informed."

"You make sure you do. I love you, Keisha."

"I love you too, Mom."

"Here, Keisha. Mom and Dad want to talk to you." Darius handed me his cell phone before I could even hang up the house phone.

"Hi, Mom."

"Hey, baby. Darius shared the good news; congratulations!" She said. "I can't believe I'm finally going to be a grandma."

"Mom, I know this isn't what you expected. I'm not even sure how it happened. It was our intention to start trying maybe a year after we were married, so I was very surprised when the doctor told me that I was pregnant. I couldn't believe it."

"Well, God doesn't make mistakes. So, we'll handle it, won't we?"

"Yes, we will. Thanks, Mom."

"You're welcome baby. Will you tell Dad for me?"

"Girl, Darius already told him. He's on the phone talking to your uncle Charles right now in the other room."

"Man, you guys sure do know how to spread news. If I ever want to get something out there fast, I'll definitely call you."

"That's not funny!"

"Just kidding, Mom. I'm glad you and Daddy are happy. Give him a hug for me and I'll call you after my next appointment. I have to go back on Tuesday."

"Yes, definitely keep us informed. I love you."

"I love you too."

I handed Darius his cell phone. He had already called both sets of parents, Jamel, Shawn, Monica, Pam and Denise. He tried to call Stacey and Steve, but they weren't at home.

"I left a message for Stacey so she could tell the rest of the family. Come here, baby."

Rubbing my hair, he kissed my forehead and then each cheek. We held each other in a tight embrace in the middle of the kitchen. Neither of us finished our dinner that night. We went to bed, not saying much to one another. I stared at him and he stared back exchanging his smile for one of mine.

"Thank you, babe. You have made me a very happy man."

"Well, that makes two of us. Two happy parents are bound to have a very happy baby."

"You got that right. My little princess will have nothing but the best."

"Hey, I thought I was your princess. Well, you just got upgraded to queen status, my love."

With my back to him, he held me close to him rubbing my stomach with both of his hands. I turned off the light and we drifted off to sleep in each other's arms, sleeping peacefully through the night. Without the sex, we were still two people in that blissful place. We had what we needed.

I awoke a couple of times during the night because of the nausea and vomiting. Only now, I wasn't annoyed. Now I understood why it was happening. We had made a baby, and this was something I was going to have to get used to for at least a few months. Each time I got up, Darius was right there with me. I'd throw up and he'd bring a bottle of Gatorade or a glass of ginger ale. He was the best thing for me. I couldn't wait to see how he faired through this pregnancy. If he was as attentive about his expectant fiancé as he was about me before he found out I was pregnant, I was in store for more love than I'd know what to do with. I wasn't complaining, though.

26 CHANGE OF PLANS

Monica left the courthouse feeling the victory of Rico's twelve-year mandatory sentence for his crimes. She hadn't slept much during the time leading up to the trial, which was evident by the dark circles surrounding her eyes. She was looking older than her years. I made a mental note to give her a jar of eye cream that would take care of that problem.

Cynthia and Monica had become quite close over the past few months and were even considering moving in together temporarily. Cynthia was in the process of having a new home built in the Waldorf area, but she'd already found a buyer for the one she currently owned. She would be living out of a hotel for a few months, otherwise. I thought it would be good therapy for both of them and by the time the house was completed, they would hopefully both be in a better place emotionally.

"You guys want to grab a bite to eat?" Cynthia signaled to make a left turn onto Route 214. "I'm starving!"

"That sounds good to me. Lately I'd been craving crab cakes and French fries. I've never really been a fan of French fries, but now I want them every day."

Monica stared out of the passenger side window with no acknowledgement of the conversation taking place in Cynthia's Navigator.

"Monica, are you okay? You haven't said a word since we left the courthouse. What's going on?" asked Shawn.

"Oh, I'm fine. I'm just glad all this mess is over. I'm a little disappointed at the sentencing, though. I really thought he deserved much more than what he got after what he did to us, but at least he's off the street for the next twelve years. He can't hurt anyone else."

"I know, I feel you one hundred percent. The system is a little messed up, isn't it?" Cynthia agreed. "It's going to be okay, though. He'll suffer in ways we may never even know about."

"You're probably right. Now what were y'all talking about?" She snapped back into her normal personality.

"We were talking about getting something to eat. You know I want my crab cakes, ladies. So, speed this thing up."

"We wouldn't want to keep a pregnant lady away from her crab cakes, now would we?" Laughing, Cynthia accelerated to make it through the traffic light that had just turned yellow."

"Girl, that traffic light has a camera on it. You'd better be careful."

"It wasn't red when I went through it. Besides, if it was, I would just tell the judge that it was an emergency."

"What emergency?"

"I'd tell him that I was in fear for my life because there was a pregnant lady in the back seat demanding that we get her to the nearest crab cake joint, or else."

"Oh, so you got jokes. Just hurry up!"

We arrived at Public House at the National Harbor before the lunch crowd and were seated immediately. Monica ordered a round of drinks to celebrate the end to the nightmare she and Cynthia had just brought to a close; ordering a virgin Pina Colada for me, of course.

"Anybody heard from Jamel lately?" asked Shawn.

"He came by last night to watch a movie. I fell asleep midway through and decided to go to bed, leaving him asleep on the couch. He cooked breakfast for me this morning and then he left," said Monica.

"That's cool. You two are getting pretty close, aren't you?"

"Jamel and I have always been cool. I don't know, it's a little odd. I mean, we do things together that couples do; but without the title. Don't get me wrong, we've never had sex or anything, but I do feel very close to him. We can talk about anything, you know how it is; Keisha."

"Sounds like Jamel wants to be more than a friend to me," joked Shawn.

"Please! I've never thought about him in any other way than that. I doubt very seriously that he wants to get involved with me after this last mess. Who wants to be with someone who's had a sexually transmitted disease?"

"Girl, you're crazy. You know how many people are running around out here who are infected with something or another and don't even tell their partners at all? Then there are those who are just like us. They caught something, but were blessed enough to be able to take antibiotics to get rid of it. Finally, there's the last group who aren't as fortunate as we were and ended up with something that there is no cure for. There are Rico's all over the place just sleeping with this one and that one and spreading nastiness around. Heck, the statistics in this car are two out of five!" Cynthia was fired up. "I doubt if Jamel looks at you any differently than he ever has. I'm sure he would never treat you like you were damaged goods. I was feeling bad about that whole thing when I first found out, but thank God it was a curable disease.

You took all of your antibiotics, right?"

"Yes, I took them all. I went back for my follow up appointment and everything is good. I'm just having a pity party right now. I'll be all right. It's just that any other time Jamel stays over, we usually share the same bed, even though we don't have sex. Last night, he was on the couch."

"Jamel is probably respecting the fact that you've been through a lot. He may think you're a little fragile and doesn't want to violate your private space. Girl, trust me. I know how he thinks," I told her. "Not to change the subject, but what do you guys think about this idea?"

"What is it, Keisha?" Pam took a break from her seafood fettuccini waiting for me to begin.

"Well, Darius and I were thinking about flying to St. Thomas to get married in six weeks. What do you guys think about that?"

"What? You mean, we're not gonna get to be a part of the union?" Shawn put her drink down and waited for my response.

"Wait a minute, let me finish! He can get some pretty reasonable tickets through some of his airport connections and we wanted all of you to come with us. The idea of a church ceremony next year went out the window with the pregnancy and all. Besides, the baby would be here and we really wanted to get married before she arrives. I know its short notice, but if you can each get the time off from work, we would love for all of you to be there. Our parents will be there along with Jamel, DJ and two of Darius's college friends. What do you think?"

"You're going to pay for everybody?" Cynthia asked, although she was certain she wasn't included in the group because she was a new friend.

"Yes, including you."

"What? So, it's like that?"

"So, what do you say? We don't have a lot of time. Your passports are all up to date, right?"

"You know it! I don't think we need them, but it's probably a good idea to have them with us," Shawn suggested.

"Girl, tell Darius to go ahead and book the tickets. Just let me know the date and I'll be packed and ready to go. That is gonna be so romantic."

"So, it's settled then."

"Wait a minute. What are we supposed to wear?"

"Well, the ceremony will take place on the beach. I've already picked out the dresses, so we'll need to go to the bridal shop sometime this week to get them. The manager over at David's Bridal said that most of the sizes in this particular dress can be bought right off the rack, but we could get a rush delivery if we needed to."

"Girl, you've got this all worked out, huh?" asked Pam.

"Well, it's not like I have a lot of time. I'll be starting to show very soon and I still want to look like a diva on my wedding day, you know what I mean? We've already applied for the marriage certificate because it'll take a couple of weeks to have the application processed. I have to make an appointment to pick it up when we get there." I pushed the plate of French fries away from me, realizing I probably needed to cut back if I was going to still look like I was in shape for the ceremony. Since finding out I was pregnant, I'd been milking it by blaming my extra food intake on the baby.

While finishing my crab cake, I visualized Darius and me standing on the beach in St. Thomas exchanging our vows. Finally, I was going to be spending the rest of my life with the man of my dreams. I thought back to less than happy times between us and silently thanked God for bringing us back where we belonged. God knew all along that we would end up back together. At that moment, I couldn't help but wonder what God must feel when He knows His people are going to have to go through some things. Those things that He allowed to happen because we stepped outside of His plan for our lives. Suddenly, I began to cry because I hurt for Him. I hurt because I knew I hadn't always done right and had disappointed God more times than I wanted to remember. This pregnancy was one of those things I knew would disgrace some; but I was in love with the father of my child and would spend the rest of my days with him. My mother reminded me that God didn't make mistakes whenever we spoke. It was as if she knew what I was feeling. Our baby was a gift from God. Wiping the tears from my eyes before my friends could notice, I exhaled and finished my crab cake. No more French fries.

27 THE ARRANGEMENTS

Darius, and the fellas picked up their suits for the ceremony. Because it would take place on the beach, they were wearing linen pant suits in a shade a little darker than ivory. We would have to have them professionally pressed once we arrived on the island, because the linen would never survive being packed in garment bags in the overhead luggage compartment of the plane. They were wearing a casual sandal-like shoe that complemented the suits very nicely. Darius picked up the tab for everything. Considering we were getting off easy by doing it this way; we wanted to make sure our friends wouldn't be put out or inconvenienced in any way financially, because of the short notice.

"Dad, I'm so glad I get to come with you to see you and Keisha get married."

"Son, I'm glad you're here too. I wouldn't have had it any other way."

Remembering DJ didn't know about the baby yet, Darius smiled. He knew his son would be so happy to have a little sibling and couldn't wait to share the news with him. Denise already knew, but vowed she wouldn't mention anything about it to their son until after the ceremony. Besides, I believed she would know when he knew because it would be all he talked about.

On the other side of town, the ladies and I were gathering our last-minute items for the trip. I still couldn't believe that we were able to pull this off on such short notice. Everything had worked out the way I planned so far for the wedding and the reception.

In just four days, I would be Mrs. Darius Kingston. We would be flying to St. Thomas in two days. There would be one day to pick up our marriage license, and get in a little relaxation before the ceremony and a week of honeymooning immediately following. Because Darius had paid for the tickets, each of our friends was able to stay for the week also. They were all willing to pick up the tab for the hotel stay, but Darius and I decided that we would take care of everything. All they needed to do was show up. I would have spent ten times the money to give everyone the opportunity to celebrate with us. They were all there through the ups and downs, the heartaches and the happiness, so they should all be there to witness the union. It was worth every penny.

I was feeling a little nauseous that day, but had gotten accustomed to an occasional episode of morning sickness. Our little bundle of joy was scheduled to arrive in five short months and Dr. Simpson; my new OB-GYN had been following my prenatal care very closely because of my Sickle Cell history. By the grace of God, I hadn't gone through a crisis in a while. I tried to remain stress free, get plenty of rest, eat healthier and stay hydrated. I was finally over my cravings of crab cakes and fries and had moved on to hitting the salad bars every chance I got, coupled with lots of dairy products, fresh fruit, nuts, chicken, and fish.

Arriving back at the house, I opened the garage door to find Darius's car parked in one of the spots. I was glad he was there.

"Hi, Love. How was your afternoon?" He asked.

"It was wonderful. I think we all have everything we need for the trip. I talked to the florist in St. Thomas to make sure the bouquets would be ready on time. The spa appointments are ready for us to get pampered the day before. The rooms are all reserved, and we have an appointment at 2:00 PM to pick up our license. Everything seems to be in order."

"Is there anything that you need me to do?"

"Just love me always."

"That's the easiest thing in the world for me to do. It's easier than breathing."

"You're so sweet, and I love you so much."

"I mean it. I love you so much that I don't know what I would do without you, Keisha. You're my sun, my moon and the stars that light up my evening sky and I love you more than you could ever know. I love you more than love, remember?"

"We'll see in a couple of months when you have to roll me through the front door."

"Baby, if you gained a hundred pounds I would love you just the same. You might not be able to get on top, but I'd still love you," he joked.

"That's not funny!"

He held me from behind caressing my stomach with both hands. Planting a kiss on either side of my neck, he held me tightly.

"I love you too."

" I heard you before."

"I wasn't talking to you," he said.

"Well who were you talking to?"

"I was talking to our baby."

I ran a bubble bath in the tub so that we could unwind after such a long day. We laid there in each other's arms looking through the skylights at the night sky. We relaxed to the sound of Baby Face singing "Someone to Love" on my favorite Pandora station. What an incredible end to an incredible day. I still couldn't believe, we were almost there.

28 THE WEDDING TRIP

We arrived at Cyril E. King Airport ten minutes ahead of schedule. The island was even more beautiful than I remembered it from my last visit. The difference this time was the love of my life was there with me and we were getting married. The guys were waiting for the luggage to come down while we rested outside on benches in front of the airport. I wasn't feeling so well, but I didn't want Darius to know because he worried too much when it came to me, especially now that there was a baby to consider. Besides, I knew it was just typical pregnancy stuff anyway.

The ride from the airport to the hotel was treacherous. The driver had to pull over twice so that I could throw up on the side of the road. I was forced to feel better when an iguana crossed my path while I was vomiting my guts out during the second stop. It scared the daylights out of me and instantly, I started to feel better. I could see Shawn laughing so hard inside the van that she was literally falling over in the seat.

"That was so funny! She cried. Whew, if you had seen your face when that thing ran by your foot? The ride in the minivan from the airport to the hotel; eighty dollars. The look on your face when you saw that iguana; priceless!" She fell out into hysterics again along with several of the others, including Darius.

"You alright baby?" Holding back his laughter, Darius rubbed the back of my neck.

"I'm fine. Did you see the size of that thing? It had to be about fifteen pounds, at least."

"I was about to get out of this van and beat it down! We're not even married yet and an iguana's trying to take my wife and child. I had your back, baby!"

"I wasn't getting out, Dad," DJ yelled from the back seat.

Immediately, there was silence throughout the van. Pam shot Darius a look that let him know he'd just opened his mouth and inserted his foot. DJ looked out the window, at a herd of goats running alongside the road. He was oblivious to what had just been revealed.

"You guys ready to have some fun?" I asked, changing the subject.

Someone needed to take control of this situation before it was too late. Denise had promised she wouldn't tell Darius Jr. about the baby, but would let us break the news to him after we were married. She kept her end of the deal, but Darius almost messed that up. I couldn't blame him, though. He had been so excited since the second I shared the news with him. I was surprised he hadn't already told DJ anyway. Besides, he was a big boy now. He probably understood more about sex and babies than we thought he did. At fourteen, he might be having sex himself. I sure hoped he wasn't.

As the van pulled into the driveway leading to the resort, there were oohs and aahs echoing from every row of seats.

The driveway to the Wyndham Sugar Bay Resort and Spa was lined with the most beautiful flowers. Some of them, we would never see outside of tropical places like this. They would never survive in Maryland.

The resort sat hidden amongst the beautiful palm trees that surrounded the mountain that it was sitting on. The sea was as clear as the beautiful diamonds in my wedding ring. Both sparkled just right when the sun hit them. St. Thomas was by far one of the most amazing islands I'd ever visited, and although we were only going to honeymoon at the resort initially; I was ecstatic when Darius agreed to get married here too. I had been to St. Thomas, but never to the resort.

During my last visit, I vowed to stay at this very location the next time I came. Who would have ever thought that I would be making lifetime memories with the love of my life in one of the world's most beautiful places. It was currently 77 degrees, which was absolutely beautiful compared to the 43 degree temperatures and rain back at home.

Once we were checked into our rooms, we all agreed to meet at the Mangrove Café for a quick lunch. I was so excited I couldn't eat, although I knew that in the best interest of our baby, I needed to put something in my stomach. I ordered a turkey and cheese sandwich on rye bread with a bowl of fruit. Picking over the meal, my mind wandered to tomorrow afternoon. I couldn't believe it was finally here. Chills ran over my body as I imagined walking across the white sand to meet my soulmate at the shoreline to become his wife. I couldn't imagine spending the rest of my life with anyone but him and was so thankful to God that we were here. Picking through the fruit, I grabbed a piece of kiwi and popped it into my mouth.

"I have to go. Darius and I have an appointment to pick up our marriage license. I scheduled appointments for spa treatments for everyone. The appointments start in a couple of hours. We should be done by that time and I'll meet you at the spa. Darius is going snorkeling with the guys once we get back. That'll give us some girl time together."

"Girl, why did you do that? You've already done so much!"

"We came here to have some fun, and fun is what we're going to have! So, let's get to it!"

"Well, I heard that!" Cynthia chanted. She grabbed her purse from the table and waited for the others to gather their things.

I walked to the pool with the ladies to get them settled before heading off to meet Darius. The pool attendant offered us drinks as soon as we walked through the entrance. Pam and Monica ordered red wine while Cynthia and Shawn decided a tropical mixed drink was more to their liking. Of course, I ended up with a glass of cranberry juice to go.

"Don't forget the little umbrella!" Shawn yelled.

"Girl, you can be so ghetto sometime," Pam rolled her eyes.

"What? It wouldn't be a tropical drink without one, now would it? Besides, for what Darius and Keisha spent on this trip, I want all the perks. My drink better have an umbrella in it!"

"This is the life!" Cynthia commented. I've never had such a wonderful time in all my life. I've been really missing out on some things. Keisha, thank you so much for inviting me."

"No problem. You're one of us now."

"I've never had friends like this before. I'm so used to doing things by myself and haven't really gotten around to getting to know anyone back in DC. Rico was the only person that I really knew besides a couple of my coworkers. I guess I was so wrapped up in him that I neglected myself and some of my own needs. You have really made me feel like a part of this group, and I want to thank you."

"You don't have to say anything else. I knew I liked you when you made it a point to introduce yourself during Rico's hearing. I'm so glad that part of your life is now over and you can pick up the pieces; you and Monica both."

"You're right." Cynthia picked up her Pina Colada. "Let's make a toast."

"Here's to lifelong relationships. May Keisha and Darius always shower each other with more love than their hearts can hold."

The cling of glasses could be heard off in the distance as I left the pool area and headed out to meet Darius in the lobby.

"Congratulations, you two! Are you ready to head to your appointment?" asked the chauffeur.

"Yes, we're very ready. Thanks!"

The appointment took less time than I thought. We were in and out of there in less than forty-five minutes, although our time slot was an hour and fifteen minutes. The day had turned out to be quite eventful. Tomorrow would be a hundred times better. We were headed back for our quality time with friends.

"I'm so ready for this snorkeling adventure. I wish you were going."

"No, I don't know if snorkeling would be a place for me in my condition. I'll go swimming with you, though. Besides, you need to spend some time with the fellas."

"You're right. Swimming sounds like a plan. Definitely after our wedding day, though. Luckily we still have a lot of time here after that."

Darius walked me to the spa entrance, kissed my forehead and headed to meet the guys. Watching him walk away, I felt so proud. Just one more day.

After leaving the spa, we all headed to our rooms to rest

for a while. I wanted to hit the beach for about an hour or so before the sun went down. A slight tan would be just what I needed to accent my wedding dress. I would wear it like an accessory for however long it lasted. As I swiped my room key, I felt butterflies in my stomach. I entered the room and headed for the sofa, where I laid for over an hour. The butterflies kept coming every few minutes. Darius came to the room to gather his wedding attire and other items that he would need for tomorrow. We decided that we would stay in separate rooms so we wouldn't see each other until the ceremony. Besides, if he stayed here with me I was afraid I would be tempted to pressure him for sex. We were getting married tomorrow, and I didn't want that to be an excuse for giving in. I wanted the anticipation of making love to my new husband to be incredible. So, for that reason, we were sleeping alone tonight.

"Darius, come here! Quick!"

"What's wrong, babe?"

"Feel this." I placed his hand over my abdomen.

Darius moved his hand slightly to the left and held it in place. "Is that what I think it is?"

"It's our baby. I started feeling her move a little while ago."

"Wow! That's amazing!" His eyes filled with tears. "I missed all of this when Denise was pregnant with DJ. Hi, little baby. It's your Daddy."

He got down on his knees and placed his ear on my stomach. Giving it a kiss, he wrapped his arms tightly around what was left of my waist. I could feel the warmth of his tears falling onto my shirt.

"Are you okay?"

"Yes, baby; I am. I'm just so happy right now that I can't control my emotions. Thank you so much!"

"What are you thanking me for?"

"You believed in me. You gave me the chance to prove that I had changed, and I am forever grateful. Now, here we are about to get married and having a baby. Life could not be any better than this."

"Darius, I always loved you. I'm sorry that I let you down when you needed me the most. You taught me how to love unconditionally. Knowing what I know now, I should have stayed before and tried to work through things with you, but I bailed out. I'm so sorry for that."

"Baby, it's okay. I understand why we broke up. I didn't at the time, but once I stopped drinking, I could see things more clearly. It wasn't until then that I realized. It's in the past now."

"You're right. It is in the past. I love you so much!"

"I love you too." Resting his head on my abdomen again, we relaxed in the moment. "Oh, and one thing, Keish. You better not tell anybody that I was in here crying like a little girl. I'll never live that down, aight?"

"Your secret's safe with me." I couldn't help but smile as I held Darius close to me.

29 THE WEDDING DAY

I awoke to a knock at the door just as the sun was beginning to shine through the window that I'd left open in the living room of my suite. *Who in the world would be knocking at this time of the morning?*

"Hey, what are you guys doing up so early?" I asked, staring at my friends through a slight opening in my right eye. The trip had taken its toll on me. I was tired and needed to rest just a little longer.

"It's your wedding day! You should be up too," said Shawn. "We came to take you to breakfast, so get dressed!"

"Can you all come back in about thirty minutes or something? I haven't even had a chance to go to the bathroom yet. Let me just take a quick shower and throw something on. I'll be down in a little while."

"You better hurry up! It'll be time for the ceremony before you know it," said Pam.

Passing by the mirror, heading toward the bathroom I knew I would need more than a couple of hours to pull that off. My hair looked like it hadn't been combed in days. Mascara residue covered the bottom of both eyelids, and there were slobber marks on my cheek and chin that resembled dried up milk on a baby's face after he'd tried to handle his sippy cup for the very first time while no one was watching. I looked a mess. There was nothing cute about me at all.

"You know what? Why don't we order room service and have breakfast out on the balcony? Besides, I don't want to risk Darius seeing me," I said, hoping they would accept my excuse to stay in.

"Girl, if he saw you right now he probably wouldn't recognize you anyway. He might even have to reconsider marrying your butt. What in the world happened to your hair?" Shawn asked, as she ran her hands through the strands, looking at them like they were dirty or smelled funny.

"You think you're so funny! Just call room service and order some breakfast. I'll be in the shower."

By the time I finished showering, washing my hair, and throwing on some shorts and a tank top, they were already devouring the eggs, sausage and toast they'd ordered. Shawn had ordered a vegetable omelet, a bowl of fresh fruit and freshly squeezed orange juice just for me. The plate was still covered in hopes of keeping some of the heat in. There was nothing worse than cold eggs.

Everything was delicious. I tried not to eat it all, because I didn't need anything extra drawing attention to my little baby bump that was already forming. Not today, anyway. It was just starting to pooch a little, so deciding to get married now was the best decision we could have made. It also meant that our baby would now be born to two loving parents who were married. She would share our last name, legitimately. Don't get me wrong, being born out of wedlock wasn't necessarily a bad thing; it just wasn't what I wanted for a child of mine and I don't believe it's what God wanted for us either.

"What time is it?" I asked. "I'm trying to figure out how much time I have to spend on my hair and make-up."

"That's why we came over. We're gonna hook you up," said Cynthia.

"I'll handle the make-up. You can take care of the hair."

I wasn't about to be walking down the beach toward my husband looking like a clown. Shawn tended to go overboard with her make-up sometimes, so I wasn't about to let her put a single make-up brush on my face. Besides, I was the make-up artist and could handle that job myself. On the other hand, she could whip some hair into shape and I trusted her with that task.

We all did our make-up and hair in my room to save time. The only thing left to do was slip into our dresses. The persimmon colored dresses complemented my gorgeous ivory colored wedding dress like the sun laying against a beautiful clear sky. They were made for each other. Darius would be pleased. We made a beautiful bridal party. I was becoming more anxious to see Darius, my one and only true love. It was time to get the show on the road.

"Keisha, you look absolutely amazing," Pam said. "I'm gonna mess up my make-up already." She dabbed at her inner eye with a tissue to keep the tears from leaving streaks on her face. "I almost forgot! Darius told me to tell you that he left something in the top of the closet for you."

"You better save those tears for the ceremony. Don't be having us all crying up in here!" Shawn threatened. "Pam! I was already trying to hold mine back.

"Please don't start, or I'll be crying too," I headed to the closet to get whatever he left there.

In the top of the closet was a beautiful jewelry box

containing the most beautiful diamond necklace I had ever seen. It was amazing! Pam placed the necklace on my neck as I looked at myself in the mirror. It was perfect for the dress and the occasion.

"Come on, let's get out of here before we all have a breakdown," I smiled at myself one last time.

We headed out the door and down into the hotel lobby where we were taking photos prior to the ceremony. The men had already been photographed on the beach. I wasn't even sure where they were at the moment, but I assumed they were somewhere getting ready for the event. After the ceremony, we would take bridal photos that included the bridesmaids and groomsmen, as well as our parents.

Stares and smiles of passersby made me feel like I'd just won the Miss Universe Pageant and was taking my celebratory walk across the stage. Two teenaged boys asked if they could take a picture with me. I agreed, but couldn't help but wonder if I would end up on social media somewhere. It was okay. They were too cute for words with their blond hair and blue eyes.

"You ladies look beautiful!" said the photographer who reminded me of Cedric the Entertainer.

"Thank you, Ced. Just make sure that we look beautiful in these pictures," said Shawn, who was receiving laughs from the crowd that had gathered to watch.

We headed toward the beach. Cynthia held the back of my dress so it wouldn't drag the ground, but most importantly; so I wouldn't trip. We decided not to wear our shoes onto the sand, and kicked them off at the edge of the trail leading to the beach. Seeing Darius off in the distance, I became anxious. I hadn't seen my Mom or my Dad since they arrived early this morning. Tony and Chris, Darius's boys from college were smiling from ear to ear as we walked toward them. Darius took a handkerchief and wiped the sweat from his bald head. We were finally face to face. People were gathering along the beach to witness the wedding. DJ stood right next to his father and looked as handsome as ever in his linen pant suit.

The ceremony began with the minister saying those things that ministers say when you're getting married. It was all a blur to me because I needed to remember the things I wanted to say to Darius before we said I do. We'd written short vows to accompany the standard vows because our lives would be based on so much more than just loving, honoring, and obeying after all we'd been through.

"Darius Kingston, if God Himself had told me that we'd be standing here today about to become one with each other, I wouldn't have believed it. We've been through some storms, but came back stronger than ever. I've loved you since our very first date and although we hit some bumps in the road our first time around, I prayed that God would bring us through; and He did. Darius Kingston; you are my sun, my moon and my stars, and I will love you until the end of our time."

There wasn't a dry eye on the beach as more people began to assemble as witnesses.

"Keisha Ayanna Johnston, I've loved you since I was fifteen years old; before I even knew you. Remember when I first laid eyes on you; I told you that you were the woman I'd been dreaming about since I was fifteen?" he smiled. "I promise to always take care of you; to protect you from harm and remain by your side," he paused, as he choked back the tears. "You are everything to me and I couldn't imagine a day without you. Keisha, I love you more than life itself, more than the sun, the moon and the stars above. By your side I will always be, I love you more . . . than love."

My mother began to sob along with Pam, Monica, Cynthia and Shawn. I even saw Chris and little DJ wipe away a tear or two. Darius was truly God's gift to me and I would cherish the words he spoke forever. I was so glad we'd decided to have the ceremony video-taped so I could watch it over and over again, and those family members who weren't present could at least experience the memory that had been captured in time.

"May we have the rings, please?" the minister asked.

Darius and I exchanged rings. He had chosen a beautiful platinum band surrounded by diamonds that fit snuggly against my engagement ring. I'd selected a larger platinum band with diamonds covering the top portion of the ring for him. We both wanted to make sure there was no question about marital status when strangers approached us in our daily comings and goings as they often did. It seemed to be an ongoing issue for us both. Only now, neither of us would have to lie about being married. We actually were.

We were finally pronounced man and wife and exchanged a long, passionate kiss on the beach in front of our friends and families, and what turned out to be about 50 spectators. Everyone began to clap as we continued our kiss. My husband scooped me up and carried me off to the gazebo where we would take the first batch of wedding photos. I felt like the luckiest woman alive. I finally had my man, I was about to have his baby, I had a new son, and the four of us were going to live happily ever after.

We took what seemed like hundreds of photos. First, there was the entire bridal party; then the parents on either side of us. There were pictures of the groom's men with the bridesmaids, and then DJ, Darius and me on the beach. There were so many combinations, I couldn't keep up. Once the pictures were all done, we went to the restaurant where we'd reserved a small ballroom space for our wedding reception. We ate, and enjoyed wedding cake before spending a couple hours on the dance floor that sat in the center of the moderately sized room. We had even invited some of the spectators from the beach to join us for the festivities.

"May I have everyone's attention for a moment?"

The sound of Jamel's fork against the wine glass sounded like wind chimes being forced by the wind to make a joyful noise.

"Keisha, I love you like you were my own sister. We have history that dates back more than fourteen years. When you met Darius, I wanted to be overprotective just to keep you safe. I worried about you when you went out on dates and wouldn't even go to sleep until I received a phone call or at least a text message letting me know you were home safely." Jamel paused.

"That's my boy!" yelled my father. Laughter filled the room.

"When you finally introduced me to Darius, I let him know from the beginning that he better not hurt you. I told him that I would be watching," Jamel pointed at his eyes and then to Darius's. Everyone began to laugh again.

"The more I got to know you, Darius, I realized that you actually had good intentions for her. You became my brother. When you told me that you would one day marry her, I knew you were serious. Now, here we are celebrating your wedding. You're a good dude and I love you, man. Please take care of my girl. I'm still watching." He laughed. "All jokes aside. You couldn't have found a better soulmate, and Keisha; you have a winner. May God bless you with more love than you can handle, lots of babies, and all the happiness in the world. To Mr. and Mrs. Darius Kingston."

"To Mr. and Mrs. Darius Kingston," said several people from the crowd.

Before long, it was time to bring the evening to a close. Mom and Dad took DJ and would be with him for the rest of the trip. I gave him a big hug and told him how much I loved him and was so happy to have him in my life. DJ would fly back to Maryland with our parents in three days so Darius and I could enjoy the rest of our honeymoon. The rest of the crew went their separate ways, but agreed to join us for a late breakfast or early lunch in the morning.

Darius wanted the best for me on the days following our wedding and the honeymoon suite was truly amazing. We bathed each other in the heart-shaped Jacuzzi tub and made love continuously. While the moon illuminated the evening sky, my new husband and I made love on our balcony; our strokes in rhythmic motion with the waves crashing against the shore. It was beautiful. Although our balcony was secluded and private, tonight I didn't worry about who might see. We were two lovers enjoying each other in the best way we knew how; but now it was different. We were husband and wife and we held nothing back.

Our lovemaking that night was like nothing that we'd ever experienced before. There was something different about making love to the man whose last name I shared. There were no inhibitions when it came to marital sex. Even in the eyes of God; He created sex to be shared between a husband and a wife and it was good! By 2:00 AM, we were exhausted. We climbed into the king-sized bed only occupying a small section. I rested my head on Darius's shoulder.

"I love you, baby." I promised.

"I love you too, my precious Angel; more than love."

I kissed him ever so gently on the lips before drifting off to sleep. It had been an exciting day and we were in store for an even more exciting life together bound by more love than we knew what to do with.

30 JAMEL & MONICA

Walking along the beach, I grabbed Monica's hand. The water rushed over and under our feet, forcing each of them to become buried in the sand. This trip had been a turning point for our friendship. We spent most of the evening in my room playing Scrabble and working crossword puzzles. Monica was very good at both, and had such a competitive spirit that she would play for hours on end because she was determined to win every game.

We ordered some light appetizers and a bottle of wine, before relaxing on the balcony.

"The sound of the ocean is beautiful, isn't it?" she asked.

"Let's go for a walk," I demanded, pulling her up from her chair.

"A walk where?" Monica asked.

"Have you looked around this place lately? This is St. Thomas! It's a beautiful island waiting to be discovered; so, get your flip flops and come on."

We ventured a couple of blocks down the road to a corner store to get something cold to drink and headed down to the beach. Monica inhaled the evening breeze as it blew through her hair. She was beautiful, and the sight of her hair blowing in the wind was beginning to do something to me. This was the sort of breeze you wished you could pack up and take home with you. Not to mention, the palm trees, tropical flowers, clear blue water and white sand. I could stay in this place forever.

This was Monica's first trip to the island, and it was important to me that she had a great time. I wanted her to enjoy it again someday, perhaps with me. I don't know, maybe the love Keisha and Darius shared was starting to rub off on me. I also wanted to find the woman of my dreams. Someone I could shower with all the love I had to give, someone I could take care of and protect. The truth is, the reason I'd never really brought anyone around my friends is because I thought one day; I would get up enough courage to let Monica know how I felt about her. I didn't want things to be awkward by bringing someone into our group who was filling a temporary void. I'd never shared this with anyone. Not even Keisha.

"Girl, you sure do walk fast. We're just walking, remember? This isn't Baltimore, and we're not trying to win a walkathon; so, would you slow it down a little?" I grabbed her hand to slow her pace.

"I'm sorry. You know I can't help it." Apologizing, she squeezed my hand tightly. "You're right, though. When we're back at home walking at night, we do walk faster, don't we?" She laughed. "You never know who or what might roll up on you in PG County, let alone, Baltimore. Isn't it beautiful out here?" she asked, inhaling the air deeply as if she was trying to ensure she didn't forget what it felt like; or what it smelled like after getting back to Maryland.

"It sure is; but not as beautiful as you looked in that dress earlier." I flirted. Monica and I had spent so much time together, but at this moment I was nervous just being next to her.

What in the world is going on here? Jamel must be tripping! I did look good, though.

"You didn't look too bad yourself," She confessed. "I mean, all of you were looking good in your suits."

"I heard there was a club not far from here; let's change clothes and go dancing," I said, changing the subject.

"You know I'm down with that. What about the others?" Monica asked. "You think we should ask them if they want to join us?"

"Well, you know Darius and Keisha won't be leaving that room any time tonight. They may not even come out tomorrow either, you know? We can ask the others if they wanna go. I think it'll be fun." I insisted, pulling her back in the direction of the resort.

"I'll see you in a little while. Just meet me at my room in 45 minutes, okay?" Monica insisted.

"All right, babe. I'll be back in a little bit. I'll check with the others to see if they wanna come, on my way to my room."

I made it back to Monica's room in 40 minutes wearing a pair of royal blue and white plaid Ralph Lauren shorts and a royal blue Polo shirt with sandals. I checked myself in the mirror across from Monica's room to make sure I looked okay, before tapping lightly on the door.

"Hey, you," she said, looking down at my toes.

"I never realized you had such nice-looking feet, Jamel," she said. "I love that outfit too. Royal blue is definitely one of your colors."

"Girl, you look good! You are wearing the heck out of that dress. It looks like it was made for you."

The short black mini dress hugged her body in all the right places. Her legs were as tone as someone who ran for leisure and not for sport. So, she still had a very feminine physique; not chiseled to the point where she looked too masculine. She was definitely sexy.

"You're looking really good," I said again.

"Thanks, Jamel. Are we the only ones going?" Monica asked, trying to change the subject.

"It looks like it. I went to Tony's room and he wasn't in. Neither were the ladies. I just assumed they might be together someplace. Who knows?"

"I wonder where they are?"

"It doesn't matter. We don't need them to have a good time, now do we?"

Jamel and Monica ended up at a club called The Zone. One of the girls at her job had told her about it after returning from her vacation six months ago. Jamel grabbed Monica's hand to guide her through the crowd, securing two seats at the bar.

"You want a drink?"

"Yeah, I'll take an Apple Martini." Reaching into her purse, she pulled out $20.

"You better put that back. I got this." I forced the $20 bill back into her purse. "Can I get an Apple Martini and a Gin and tonic?" I asked the bartender.

We sat at the bar and finished our drinks. Realizing that Monica was a little tense, I ordered a second Martini for her.

"Let's dance." Grabbing her hand, I led her to the dance floor.

We danced until there wasn't a single curl left in her hair, but she was still so sexy! Monica pulled a band out of her purse and pulled her hair up loosely on top of her head. She turned her back to me and began dancing closely against my body. The blood began to rush from my head throughout my body in a couple of minutes. I pulled away, so she wouldn't be alarmed by the affect she was having on me. I hadn't had sex in a while, so I was a little embarrassed for her to know that the slightest touch of her body had aroused me. Trying to shake the feeling, I began thinking about something other than the way her body moved against mine. Something that would take this feeling away, at least for now. I guess thinking about the scent of her perfume didn't help either. There it was again. This thing better behave before it gets us both into something we can't get out of.

Monica and I danced until 4:00 o'clock in the morning before heading back to the hotel. I placed my arm over her shoulder during the cab ride, and placed her head on my chest. She was asleep in a couple of minutes. My heart got the best of me and I planted a kiss on her forehead, brushing the strands of hair that were dangling in her face gently behind her ear.

I couldn't help but think about the fragile state that she still might be in after going through her ordeal with Rico, but I really wanted her. I wanted her more than I'd ever wanted any woman, though there hadn't been that many. I'd never had the nerve to express this to her before. I believed tonight was the night. Before we arrived back at the hotel, I would figure out how I was going to tell her. It's funny how being in paradise had a way of making people do some crazy things. I guess it was my turn, although I knew I wasn't just caught up in the moment. The atmosphere had not taken over. I was really feeling her and always had.

"Jamel, I had such a good time! Thanks for taking me," she said, with a large smile on her face.

"Baby, you know me. I aim to please."

"You wanna come in? She asked?

"Yeah, why not?" I smugly said because I didn't want her to know how anxious I was to spend more time with her.

She walked toward the sliding glass to open the door leading out to the balcony. Like a little puppy, I followed her.

"This is so amazing. I could sleep right out here."

I placed my body against her back, wrapped my arms around her waist and held her close to me. She looked over her shoulder and into my eyes before turning her body to face mine. The silence between us was like the calm after a bad storm, so peaceful. My lips wanted to reach out to her, to kiss her so gently and with passion at the same time. I thought back to all the times Monica had spent the night at my house, slept in my bed; but nothing happened because of the respect I had for her. Right now, it was all about to be a distant memory.

"What are you thinking about?" she asked.

Smiling, I let my lips explain by kissing her once very softly. Then again on the right side of her neck. I held her body in a tight embrace. The sound of her exhaling confirmed that it was okay. I didn't want to let her go, but I wouldn't make the first move. If anything were going to happen between us tonight, it would be on her terms.

"Jamel," she said.

"Yes, babe, what's up?"

"Can you stay here with me tonight? I don't want to sleep alone."

She grabbed my hand and guided me to the bedroom of her suite. After taking off her shoes, she turned around for me to unzip her dress. I obliged. Her hourglass figure was a complement to the burnt orange colored bra and panty set she wore. It matched her bridesmaid's dress perfectly. She was more beautiful than any Victoria's Secret model I'd ever seen because she was real. She had black girl curves.

I removed my shorts and shirt before stepping into Monica's personal space. I wanted to hold her, make love to her tonight and many more nights. I wanted to love her forever. Placing her on the bed, I rested my body gently on top of hers. The warmth of her body forced my body to respond, but this time it was okay. I wasn't embarrassed anymore. Our bodies were in agreement of what we were about to do. No matter how far we went, it would mean more to me than she would ever know.

"Take off your boxers," she whispered.

"Are you sure?" I asked while removing them.

"She unhooked her bra and laid it on the nightstand.

Then she removed her panties and for the first time ever, the two of us were basking in our nakedness with no shame, no embarrassment, or regrets. I'd never seen her like this before.

"I want to touch you so badly," she said.

"Don't talk. Just do it," I whispered in her ear.

Monica reached out and touched my bare chest. She then ran her fingers down to my stomach. Then she hesitated. I reached into the pocket of my shorts for one of the two condoms I'd put in my wallet before leaving my room, but I didn't open it. I put it on the nightstand.

Monica kissed my lips, then rested her head on my shoulder. I wanted to make the early morning hours of this day last forever. We held each other to the sounds of Ne-Yo playing on her iPhone in the background. It was the perfect song for our first physical encounter together, and although we didn't make love; we were seeing each other in ways we never had before. It was enough for me. I had so much respect for her, that it was okay; and although we were both naked, I didn't disrespect her in any way. There would be plenty of time for us to experience each other in that way. This just wasn't it.

I woke up at sunrise and smiled when I realized she was really there. While Monica rested, I ordered room service. I wanted to feed her before we started our day.

"Good morning, sleepy head. I ordered breakfast."

"Wow, you didn't have to do that," she said.

Monica took a bite out of one of the strawberries and placed the other half in my mouth.

"Come on over here and sit down. You need to eat more than that," I helped her out of bed and over to the table I'd set for two. "Why are you smiling?"

"Because no one has ever treated me like this before," she admitted.

"Are you serious? Every man you've ever dated should have been treating you this way. You've been getting cheated," I told her.

"You're such a gentleman," she moved from her chair and onto my lap.

"You deserve one of those, you know?" I hinted. "A gentleman, that is."

We finished breakfast with her sitting in my lap, feeding me turkey sausage, eggs, and wheat toast with mixed tropical fruit. She was wearing nothing but her burnt orange panties and my royal blue Polo shirt. After the plate was empty, she headed for the shower.

"Why don't you join me," she teased.

We showered together, and although it took every ounce of self-control I had not to do anything crazy; I enjoyed the shower more than any other shower I'd ever taken. The truth is, I was in love with her. She just didn't know it. Or maybe she did.

"I guess I better head to my room to put on some fresh clothes," I said.

"Do you have plans for today?" she asked.

"No, but I was hoping that you would spend the day with me. Do you have anything going on?"

"No, but I think Keisha and Darius wanted us all to have lunch with them early this afternoon."

"That sounds good to me, but I'd like to take you for another walk later. Maybe we could head out into town for a little shopping this evening, that is if you want to," I suggested.

"Yes, that definitely sounds like a plan. Maybe right after lunch we can go out. Jamel, thank you for being who you are."

"You don't have to thank me for anything."

"I feel like I do. I have a confession to make. I've been checking you out for years, but I didn't think I was your type. I feared the rejection, so I never said anything. I've never done more than hint around to Keisha about it, but I never came out and told her."

"Wow! You're not gonna believe this, but I've felt the same way for a while myself. I was afraid to tell you, and after what happened between you and Rico; I figured it would be a while before I would be able to. I didn't want to put any pressure on you after all of that, but I wanted to be there for you as more than just a friend. Can I ask you something?"

"You can ask me anything," she looked intently into my eyes.

"Where do we go from here? I mean, I'm not the type of guy to just go around having casual sex with women, especially one that I care so much about. One that I love. I guess you can see that after last night. We spent the entire night naked, and it took everything in me not to try to make love to you, but I respect you more than anyone I've ever known. What now?" I asked. "Wait, don't answer yet. I really want to take this to the next level. I want to be in a committed relationship . . . with you."

"Jamel, I would love to be in a committed relationship with you. I'll check a box, say yes; whatever you want me to do," she laughed.

"Let me get dressed and I'll come to your room with you so that you can do the same. I'll just bring my makeup bag over there.   It looks like I'm going with this wash-n-go hairstyle today, so I just have to put some coconut oil and moisturizer on it.   I can do that in your room, if you don't mind."

"You can do whatever you want, babe."

As we walked to my room, I envisioned a bathroom vanity with double sinks. Monica is in the mirror doing her hair and applying her makeup while I'm shaving on the side that occupies my personal effects. We're in our own home somewhere in PG County. Maybe out in Bowie or another part of Upper Marlboro. I could see our future. The one we would start building from this day forward.

31 MIND YOUR BUSINESS

The gang all gathered for an early lunch in the hotel's dining room at 11:30. Darius and Keisha came down hand in hand with smiles plastered on their faces.

"Wow! What are y'all smiling about?" Shawn joked. "Must have been some good honeymoon love making going on up there."

"Don't hate," Darius joked, pulling his new wife closer to his side.

"Keisha, come here for a minute. Darius, do you mind if I borrow your wife for a second?" Shawn asked.

"What's up?" Keisha put her hands on her hips.

"Girl, I was walking past Monica's room early this morning and I swear, I think she had some man up in there," Shawn whispered.

"You're crazy! What, you think she came down here and met some island boy? Her name ain't Stella!" Keisha laughed.

"I'm serious, Keisha. I heard a couple of moans and then some laughter. I'm gonna ask her about it." Shawn said.

"You better mind your business. If she met somebody

and had sex with him, she'll either tell us about it; or she won't, because she already knows what we're going to say. How could she come down here and just have sex with some random guy? No! Think about it, Shawn; after what she just went through with Rico, do you really think she'd be that stupid? I don't believe she did anything like that." Keisha was disgusted. "Why'd you have to go and ruin my morning? I'm going to forget you said that."

Keisha took her seat next to Darius at the table. Rolling her eyes at Shawn, she almost fell out of her chair when Monica and Jamel exited the elevator and headed in their direction.

"Good Morning. Where are you two just coming from?" Keisha asked.

"We're just coming down from the room." Monica said. "Jamel took me dancing last night over at The Zone. We had the time of our lives. We didn't get back here until early this morning."

Immediately, Shawn shot Keisha a look that said something she had not thought about. *Monica and Jamel spent the night together! She was the man that Shawn heard her having sex with this morning. What in the heck is going on here?*

"So, y'all done came down here and made a love connection?" Shawn asked.

"Shawn, you need to mind your business!" Jamel defended Monica. He knew that they would all find out soon enough, but he didn't feel their best friends' honeymoon was the time or the place.

The entire table went silent. No one else said a word about Jamel or Monica. Everyone just enjoyed their food. In the back of Keisha's mind, she made a mental note to get the 411 from Monica later. If she wanted to have sex with Jamel, that was her business. She just prayed they both knew what they were getting into. Jamel was one of Keisha's dearest friends, and she didn't want to see him get hurt. They'd had numerous conversations about relationships and it was a known fact that Jamel wanted to eventually settle down once he found the right woman, of course. He was looking for a wife. He wanted to have kids. Monica was a good friend too, and really needed a good man in her life. What Keisha had to admit was they were both consenting adults. If they wanted to have sex or be in a relationship, that was their business. She just wanted them to be serious about it so neither one of them ended up hurt.

After breakfast, they changed into their bathing suits and went jet skiing. Ironically, Monica ended up on the back of a jet ski with Jamel. She wrapped her arms around his waist so tightly; it almost looked like the two of them were glued together. Shawn was not going to take her eyes off those two.

Something is going on here and I'm going to find out what it is. I mean, if she wants to be with Jamel; I guess that's her prerogative. I ain't mad at her because Jamel is fine. I always thought he was going to end up with Keisha, but now she has her man. Oh well, I guess Monica and Jamel are a couple. Either that or they're just sleeping together. That's probably all it is. Why do I care anyway? I have got to find myself a man! I've got way too much time on my hands.

32 WE BELONG TOGETHER

"Man, I wasn't expecting to get that type of reaction out of them, were you?" Jamel asked Monica as they walked together toward the Gucci store on Yacht Haven Grande. "Do you think Keisha was disappointed when she saw us?"

"No, I don't think she was disappointed. Maybe disappointed at that ghetto acting Shawn, but not at us," he laughed.

"Yeah, you're probably right."

"Jamel, what are we doing in here? This stuff is way outside of my budget. I only own one, and Keisha actually bought that one for my birthday two years ago during one of their sale events."

"It's not over my budget. What do you think of this?"

Jamel handed Monica one of the bags from Gucci's summer collection. A large red hobo.

"It's nice and roomy. Yeah, I like this a lot."

"I'll take one of these and the matching wallet," Jamel told the sales associate.

"Jamel, what are you doing?"

"I'm buying you a gift."

"A $2,200 purse? And a $600 wallet?"

"Yes, is there something wrong with that? Listen, if you're gonna be with me, you better get used to it. I want you to have it. You look good in red and it's your favorite color. This bag is calling your name."

"Would you two like a bottle of cold water while I get your package ready?" the associate asked.

"Yes, we would love some. Thanks," said Jamel.

"Wow, babe! Thank you so much! I really love it!"

"You're welcome, sweetheart. Only the best for you."

"You're not going to get anything?"

"I have everything now that I have you. I don't need anything else."

Monica kissed Jamel softly on his lips. She wrapped her arms around his neck and held him in a tight embrace. As she stepped away, she saw Shawn, Cynthia, and Pam walking by the store.

"There's nosy. She probably saw us."

"I don't really care if she did. I'm gonna tell Darius and Keisha as soon as we get home anyway. Besides, we're two adults and can make our own decisions about who we date, who we love, or anything else."

"I heard that, babe."

The sales associate, they later found out was called Miranda handed them the package with two more bottles of water for the walk. The two of them left. Monica held Jamel's hand with one of hers while he carried her new Gucci wallet and purse in the shopping bag.

"You need anything, love?" He asked.

"No, I don't need anything."

"Well, I guess we better head back."

"Yes, I'm a little tired. I think I need to take a nap before we catch up with everyone later this evening."

"Yes, let's do that. Are we napping separately or together?" Jamel asked.

"What do you think? You can't get rid of me now."

The two of them walked slowly back to the hotel, engaging in various conversations from the comedic to the most intimate. They were definitely made for each other. It's funny that it took so long for them to get to a place they were destined to be, but I guess it was all about timing. Nothing that a little liquid courage and tropical scenery couldn't jump start.

Jamel and Monica laid across the bed under the ceiling fan with the cool island breeze blowing in from the patio door and living room window. Monica stood and removed her sundress before laying back on the bed. Jamel took off his shorts and t-shirt.

"Come here, beautiful."

Monica crawled over to the spot where Jamel rested on the bed. She straddled his body and began massaging his chest. Instantly, he became aroused; but he put the thoughts in the back of his mind. He knew that she wanted him too. He could feel it in more ways than one.

"Let's just lay here," she said.

"Yes, we can do that."

"Jamel, are you sure you're okay with this? I mean, I am asking for a lot by expecting you to be around me like this and not do anything."

"Baby, I wouldn't have it any other way. Whatever happens between us, I want it to happen in the right time and the right way. We don't have to force anything. With or without sexual intimacy, I'm going to be here for you."

"You're the best, babe."

"Monica, I'm your fair-weather friend trying to be the one constant in your life that will never hurt you, leave you lonely, break your heart, or anything like that. I just want to love you. I just want to enjoy this ride. Just the two of us."

The sun went down on their half naked bodies sprawled across the bed. They loved each other without ever touching at all. They were loving each other with their minds, which was more powerful than anything either of them had ever experienced before. He couldn't help but think of how much he was enjoying their time together in St. Thomas, but he couldn't wait to get her home. Before long, he would be convincing her to give up her apartment to take up residency in his house. There was plenty of room for them both, and it would save her quite a bit of money. He knew she needed a new car and now she would be able to get it, although he was probably going to put a large down payment on it to keep her payments low. The way things were going; he might even buy it.

"Oh, Jamel. What are you trying to do to me?"

"Trying to love you. That's it."

He rested his head on her stomach and stared into her eyes. He reached for her left hand and smiled. In a year, he could see a big diamond ring on it. Jamel would plan the most romantic proposal that his mind could conceive. That's just the way he was. Unfortunately, there weren't many women who had experienced what he had to offer. Jamel was very selective in who he dated. He'd always been that way. So, for him to make a commitment to Monica, everyone would know that she was the woman he'd fallen in love with and would surely marry.

"So, what's going to happen when we get back home? I mean, we're here in paradise and it's all fine and good. Are you still going to feel the same way about me when we get back to Maryland?" Monica asked.

"Girl, I thought you knew me better than that. How many women have you seen me with since you've known me?" He asked.

Jamel had a point. Monica had only seen him with maybe two women in the past eight or more years, and it was by accident that she saw him. He never brought anyone around their circle of friends. He introduced Michelle as his girlfriend, but five months later; she was gone. He found out she was cheating with a man almost twice her age. Michelle had told Jamel that the other man was her Sugar Daddy and she only relied on him to pay her car note and rent. Jamel was so disgusted with her that he ended the relationship immediately. Right after that, he had what he called the "no gold digger" policy. With that said, he spent a lot of time alone. Jamel was making excellent money and had a lot going for himself. Women saw that and wanted to dig their claws in, but Monica was never like that. This was part of the reason why he was so attracted to her, because she saw him and not what he had to offer.

"Monica, when we get back to Maryland; we're gonna start working toward our future together. You deserve so much more than you've gotten in past relationships. I want to show you how a woman is supposed to be treated. I've always had your back, but now I have your back, side, front, everything. Just let me take care of you."

"Babe, that's so sweet. I love you."

"And I love you to the moon and back. We have been through some things together, haven't we?"

"How many nights did you sleep next to me in my bed because we stayed up too late watching movies for you to drive home? How many times did we go to the movies, out to dinner or to the club? When you think about it, what in the world were we doing? They all sound like dates to me!" She reminisced.

"I know, right? Remember that time we went to H2O and that guy was pulling on your arm while we were walking to get a drink?" He laughed.

"Yeah, I remember that. He was so drunk, it wasn't even funny!" She remembered. "We've always had a good time together. I miss Club H2O. We have a lot of memories from that place. Wow! We've known each other for a long time!"

"Yes, we have. I remember, that dude pissed me off when he grabbed your arm. I was gonna rip his head off. That made me jealous, but I tried not to let it show. I mean, here we are walking through the club together, trying to make it through the crowd; and this dude grabbed your arm. How did he know that you weren't my lady? I was holding your hand!" Jamel's emotions took over as if he was back at H2O that very night.

"Yeah, I know. It was disrespectful. But you best believe; nobody else got out of line that night. They probably thought they'd be facing a serious butt whipping if they even looked at me wrong," she laughed. "You sure had my back."

"That's my point. I will always have your back. You're my lady now and that means even more to me than anything else. It's my job to protect you and to make sure that you're safe. Trust and believe. When that happened between you and Rico? That didn't sit well with me; but it wasn't my place to do anything. Well guess what, baby girl? It is now." He promised.

Monica rested her head on Jamel's shoulder as they lounged in the hammock on the balcony of the room. Lately, they'd only occupied one although two rooms had been paid for. When they returned home, they agreed to share the news of their relationship with everyone. But for now, they wanted to continue to get to know each other on a more intimate level. Before getting ready to meet for dinner, they held each other for another hour. The truth is, they were already trying to think of an excuse to leave dinner early. They wanted to spend as much time together, alone as they could.

"I'll tell you what. We'll just eat a light dinner and make an excuse to leave. We can always order something if we get hungry later."

"That sounds like a plan to me." Monica smiled.

33 THE VISIT

"Darius, baby. Would you get the door?" I yelled from the bathroom sink area. After washing my hands, I headed in the direction of the foyer.

"It's Jamel and Monica!" Darius yelled back.

"Hey, what brings you two to our happy home? We haven't seen or heard from either of you since we got back almost a month ago. What's up with that?" Darius asked.

"Man, where's Keisha?"

"She's just coming out of the bathroom. Why, what's going on?"

"Nothing. We just wanted to talk to the two of you about something. So, how's married life?" Jamel changed the subject. He only wanted to have to say it once, so he was waiting for Keisha to come into the family room.

"Man, it's all that and then some! I mean, I've been with this woman for a while; but now that we're married, it's almost like everything is magnified. The love making is crazy! I just can't keep my hands off her, and I don't know what it is about pregnancy, but man! I gotta have her 24/7. It's almost like we've never done it before. Now that we're married, we can't stop!"

"Darius! Did you forget that I was sitting here?" Monica reminded him.

"Oh. Sorry, Monica. I'm just keeping it real, girl."

"I'm just kidding. I definitely understand," Monica smiled.

"What are you talking about baby?" Keisha asked while walking into the room on the tail end of the conversation.

"Nothing, babe." Darius and Jamel laughed.

"What are you two doing here?" Keisha asked. She bent down and gave her friends a hug.

"We just stopped by to see what you two were up to. We just came from the bowling alley and thought we'd stop by to see how you were feeling." Monica said.

"Girl, I've been feeling pretty good. I'll be so glad when this baby is born. I didn't know that my body could stretch in so many different directions. She's moving around a lot."

"That's great! I can't either. We're all waiting to welcome the newest family member. She's gonna have so many aunties, it's not even funny!"

"Can I get you guys something to drink?"

"How about a couple bottles of water?" Jamel asked.

Keisha returned from the kitchen and handed each of them an ice-cold bottle. She sat down and began drinking hers like she'd just escaped from the desert where she thought she would die from heat exhaustion and dehydration.

Sitting in the family room exchanging glances across the room, Monica and Jamel sat on the love seat trying to break the ice so they could announce the news.

"Man, let me just say it. Keisha and Darius; Monica and I have something to tell you."

"Go ahead, what's up?" Keisha asked. She already had an idea of what he was about to say, but tried not to let on.

"Well, Monica and I have been seeing each other."

"So, what else is new?" asked Darius.

"What do you mean, what else is new?"

"Man, Stevie Wonder could have seen that one coming! I knew it when we were in St. Thomas. Ya'll must think we're slow or something. I've been peeping that out for a minute now. Keisha and I were wondering how long it was gonna take for you to fess up." Darius laughed.

"Keisha, why didn't you say something?" Monica asked.

"Girl, it wasn't my business. Besides, after Shawn put you on blast in St. Thomas, I figured I better leave it alone. I knew when you were ready to tell, you would.

"So, you're not upset about it?" asked Monica.

"Girl, please. You both know how I feel about you. I just want the two of you to be happy and to take care of each other. What's funny about the whole thing is I always wondered why you didn't get together. I know how close you are. I just assumed that you had at least slept together years ago. I know Shawn said she heard you two in the room early one morning when she was passing by, because she told me. At the time, she didn't know it was Jamel in there with you. She thought you had met some island boy and sexed him up while our backs were turned," Keisha said in her best Caribbean accent.

"She probably had her ear glued to the door, with her nosy self! You know how she is. But for real, we never slept together. Well, not exactly. Let's just say we were never intimate in any way until St. Thomas. Love was definitely in the air, wasn't it?" Monica daydreamed back to the trip to St. Thomas. "It was truly an amazing time for us all, and it's because of you that Jamel and I sit here now."

"She told me she saw you at the Gucci store too. That girl doesn't miss much. I like that bag. I have that one in another color, but the red is hot! Alright, Jamel! You always did have excellent taste."

"I'm glad you approve," he said.

They talked for another hour until they were interrupted by the doorbell again. Neither of them was expecting a visitor, although they weren't expecting Monica and Jamel either. Keisha walked towards the door as the doorbell rang a second time. Peeking through the glass panel to the left of the door, she hesitated before opening it.

"I don't know who this is. Darius, come here a second!" she yelled.

As Darius walked toward the door, he peeked through the panel as well. They lived in a very safe neighborhood, but you never knew what kinds of crazy people might be lurking around.

"What the hell?" Darius said as he opened the door.

"Well it's about time I caught up with you!" the woman said who was now trying to push her way through the front door.

"Hold up! Stephanie, what are you doing here?" Darius asked.

"Stephanie? I know this isn't that chick you were telling me about, is it?" Keisha huffed. "What in the hell are you doing standing on our porch? I thought she was in Atlanta?" Keisha looked at Darius for an answer.

"Stephanie, what are you doing here? Didn't I make myself clear when I told you that I was getting married?"

"I know what you said; but I didn't believe you would do that to me."

"Stephanie, we only had sex once and I'm so sorry that I even went there with you. Please leave us alone! My wife is pregnant and we do not need this drama. When Keisha and I decided we were getting back together, I told you the truth about that. Hell, you and I hadn't seen each other in five or six months before that and now you're showing up on my doorstep? What is up with that? Are you crazy? Don't make me step outside myself, Stephanie!"

Jamel and Monica headed toward the front door for reinforcement just in case Stephanie tried something. There was no way Darius was going to let her anywhere near his wife. She'd never get within arm's reach of Keisha before he did what he had to do to defend her and his unborn baby. He didn't have a pattern of putting his hands on women, but he would if it were a matter of protecting his wife. Monica didn't even want to put him in that position. She could take care of Stephanie if she had to.

"This chick better get out of here before I forget I'm pregnant! Get off this porch right now and take your drama back to Georgia before I beat the hell out of you!" Keisha yelled.

Darius held her back. All the while, Stephanie was standing on the porch with a deer in the headlights look on her face.

"Look, Stephanie. You need to leave. I don't ever want to see you again and definitely don't have anything to say to you. I don't owe you anything. I'm happy in my life with my beautiful wife who is about to have my baby in just a few months, so you need to get out of here and head back to wherever it is you came from."

"Bastard, you can talk that mess all you want to, but you know you want this!" Stephanie's slurred speech and the smell of alcohol on her breath were evidence that she was at least a little intoxicated.

"Please! I didn't want it when I had it the first time. You were merely someone who filled a night of loneliness when I was missing this woman right here! I'm sorry I slept with you, but you need to let that go! It meant absolutely nothing! You knew that back then!"

"We'll see about that. We'll see who you call when your WIFE leaves you! You don't want her! You know you want me! She ain't even all that cute anyway! So what if she light skinned with pretty hair! She is not all that!"

"Stephanie, do you know how stupid you sound? If you don't get your ugly butt off this property, I swear I'm gonna beat you so bad you won't even remember driving over here! In fact, you need to leave before PG County gets here because I just called them!" Monica yelled. "My girl is pregnant, and I'll be damned if I'm gonna let you come over here and disrupt their happy home like this! Now get out of here!"

Just as Monica threatened Stephanie one final time, sirens could be heard coming through the neighborhood. Stephanie tried to run to her car, but didn't make it before PG County PD pulled up. She was questioned and placed in the back of one of the police cars. She was detained once the officers found out that she was wanted back in Atlanta for domestic assault. A search of the rental car revealed a Glock 9MM handgun, two knives and two pairs of latex gloves. Not to mention, she failed the breathalyzer. It appears that Stephanie came all the way to Maryland to really hurt somebody.

The following morning, Darius and Keisha took out a restraining order against her just in case she decided to show her face again. Talk about drama; but Keisha had a feeling it was coming sooner or later anyway. She was just waiting for it, and here it was. One thing's for certain, Keisha was a true lady but she could go hard for those she loved. She and Darius had come too far to have some crazy, psycho, stalker type come along and ruin it. For now, she was pregnant but after the baby was born, if she had to take some sort of action to defend herself against Stephanie; she knew what to do.

34 LIFE WILL NEVER BE THE SAME

(Four months later). When Keisha reached Darius on his cell phone, she could barely get the words out of her mouth.

"Baby, I need you to come home," she said in a panic.

"What's wrong babe? You miss Big Daddy?"

"Big Daddy better get home right now!" she yelled. "I'm in labor!"

"Wait, what? I'm on my way!" Darius headed down from the tower. "My wife's having the baby!" He yelled while heading out the door. Darius could hear cheers and claps as he ran toward his car. Looking back, he could see his boys still cheering him on as they watched him through the window. Driving down 395, Darius hit speeds of 85 mph. He prayed he didn't get stopped, because he would only have to break the law again after the ticket was issued. There was no way he could drive the speed limit right now. Keisha was at the house in pain, and with her health condition he didn't want to risk anything. She needed to be at the hospital where there were specialists to deal with the labor and the Sickle Cell to make sure that there weren't any problems with the delivery. Pulling into the driveway, Keisha was waiting at the front door. Darius could tell that she was in a substantial amount of pain. Jumping out of the car, he headed toward her and gave her a big hug.

"Hey, beautiful; where's your suit case?" He asked, but realized that it was on the floor right next to where she stood.

"I'm so glad you made it. This hurts!" she yelled.

"Come on, Mommy. We need to get you to the hospital and fast. You need to grab anything out of here before I lock up?" he asked.

"No, I think I have everything. Just remember to put the baby's car seat in the car before you pick us up from the hospital once we get released." She reminded.

"I'll remember." He said. "Did you call our parents to tell them you were in labor?" He asked.

"No, I haven't called anyone yet. I've been so busy trying to get through these contractions. Can you call them once we get in the car?"

"You're right, Sweetheart. I'll have time to make a couple of calls once I get you checked in. Right now, I need to focus on getting you to the hospital, safely. Besides, my nerves are gonna be shot to hell while I wait for them to get you ready," he admitted.

Backing out of the driveway, Mr. and Mrs. Kingston headed to the hospital to give birth to their very own baby daughter. Darius was as nervous as he could be.

Once they arrived, a nurse came out with a wheel chair to transport Keisha into the hospital. She was so thankful she'd pre-registered and didn't have to sit for thirty minutes giving information that she knew they already had. Keisha and Darius were in labor and delivery before they knew it. After twenty-seven pushes, their baby daughter made her way into the world at seven pounds and one ounce. Little Keyana was in her daddy's arms while the tears flowed down each of his cheeks. He held her close to his heart, giving her a gentle kiss on her nose; he thanked God for giving them the gift of a beautiful, healthy baby girl. Darius sat down on the edge of the bed and placed baby Keyana in Keisha's arms so they could begin the bonding process.

Just as tears began to fall down Keisha's cheeks, both sets of parents walked in. There were so many balloons, teddy bears and flowers that Keisha's room now looked like a flower shop. Darius remained in a daze as he played back the events of the delivery. He still couldn't believe that God had blessed him with the beautiful wife that almost slipped away; and now a precious baby girl. Darius loved Keisha more than love; and now he had two of them to love more than he could describe in words. God was so good!

The rest of the crew showed up just in time to see the baby before Darius laid her down to rest. She looked like a little angel.

"Oh, my God. She is absolutely beautiful," said Monica. "She's got a head full of beautiful curls and a little button nose just like you, Keisha!"

"Yes, she is amazing; isn't she?" Keisha admitted. "She's going to be spoiled rotten."

This was the first baby in the family since Darius Jr. was born, and my parents were first time grandparents. My dad was already talking about setting up a college fund.

"Well, ya'll just let me know when you need a babysitter," Shawn offered. "I'll be happy to watch her so you can get out when you feel up to it."

Keisha knew in the back of her mind that it would be a long while before she would leave Keyana with anyone. She already knew she was going to be out of work for twelve weeks and her mother was going to watch her once she returned to work, at least until she was old enough to talk. Neither of them wanted to risk anything happening to her and felt comfortable knowing that she would be with family.

They had even discussed Keisha leaving the workforce for a while, if that's what she wanted to do. Darius was making more than enough money to support the family.

The group was so engaged in conversation about the beautiful baby and what features she inherited from which parent that they hadn't even notice the woman lurking outside the hospital room door. Monica excused herself and left the room, heading down the hallway in her direction.

"What in the hell are you doing here?" she asked. "You must really want me to whip you real bad! I know I told you that it was gonna happen if you didn't stay away from my friends. What part of that didn't you understand?"

Keisha looked at Darius when she heard Monica's slightly elevated voice outside in the hall. He and Jamel left the room to see what the commotion was all about, though they both suspected who it was.

It was Stephanie. This chick was going to be a problem. She rolled her eyes at Darius and headed toward the elevator. Darius called 911 to have her picked up. She obviously didn't care about the restraining order and he was not about to let her get close to his wife or his daughter. He would protect them, by any means necessary. In his mind, he wondered what he had done. He had opened his world to a crazy stalker who obviously wasn't getting what he was trying to say. He never thought he'd ever come face to face with a stalker type, and he was about to find out just how crazy she was. He had attached himself to the wrong person.

PART II

(A SNEAK PEEK)

Monica got out of her car and headed toward Keisha and Darius's front door. She knocked three or four times and waited for Keisha to answer. *Something's wrong. I just spoke to her an hour ago. She knew I was on my way over.* Standing on the porch, she dialed the house phone but there was no answer. The cell phone went unanswered too. *What in the world is going on?*

"Jamel, it's me," her voice shook with panic. "I just got over to Keisha and Darius's place, but Keisha's not answering. She knew I was on my way over here, so I'm concerned."

"What? Let me call Darius. Maybe she and the baby had to run out?" said Jamel.

Monica rested her arm on the front door while waiting for Jamel to come back to the line. The door creaked. It was open.

"Babe, Darius said he talked to her a little over an hour ago. She didn't say anything about going out. In fact, he said she told him you were on your way over there," now Jamel was in a panic too.

"Babe, the door is open. I'm going inside. Stay on the line with me, please?" she begged.

"Darius is on his way home. I'm on my way over there too. Maybe you better wait until I get there before going in."

"Jamel, no! You know I won't be doing that. My best friend and our Goddaughter might be in trouble. I'm going in now!" she demanded.

"Keisha? Keisha, are you okay?" Monica yelled as she entered the large foyer area.

Suddenly, she could hear Keyana crying from her nursery. Monica ran up the stairs and into the baby's room. There was Keyana lying in her crib with her face as red as sunburned skin. Her diaper was so wet that her sleeper and mattress cover were soaked. She had obviously been lying there for a while with no one to see after her. She picked up the baby and walked to Keisha and Darius's room. Keyana was now whimpering.

There on the floor was Keisha. She appeared to be dead, but the rise and fall of her chest confirmed that she wasn't.

"Oh my God, Jamel! I found her! She's unconscious on the bedroom floor!" she screamed while trying to console the baby at the same time.

She placed Keyana in the center of the king-sized bed and grabbed the bedroom phone from the base to call 911.

"Hello, I need and ambulance at 125 Hickory Street in Upper Marlboro! Please hurry!"

"What's the nature of your emergency, Ma'am?" asked the 911 operator.

"My friend is lying on the floor unconscious! Her baby's here and It looks like she's been crying for a while, please hurry!"

"I have someone on the way. Does she have a pulse?"

"Yes, she's breathing but non-responsive."

"Does her baby appear to be okay?"

"Yes, I believe so."

While Monica communicated with the 911 operator, she heard something coming from Keisha's closet. She placed the phone on the nightstand and reached for Darius's gun that was in the drawer. Thrusting the closet door open, she saw a figure dressed in dark clothing hunched in the corner of the closet.

"Who in the hell are you? What are you doing here?"

There was no response from the person who was obviously an intruder. Suddenly, the dark figure lunged toward Monica, grabbing her around the neck. The two struggled for what seemed like forever. In the background, Monica could hear Keyana crying again. They continued to struggle. Then suddenly, a loud pop echoed through the room. Keyana's crying intensified. The dark figure fell to the floor, struggling to survive. Monica snatched off the mask and looked the intruder in the eye.

"Stephanie! What have you done? Monica cried."

Monica could hear the sound of sirens heading in the direction of the house. Then finally, there was silence. Keyana had stopped crying, Stephanie was no longer moving, and the paramedics were on their way up the stairs. Monica ran back toward the phone.

"Please send the police. I've shot someone!"

"The police should already be on route, Ma'am. Who is the person you shot?"

"Her name is Stephanie Morgan. She's been stalking this family for over a year now."

"Is she still breathing?"

Monica guided the paramedics to Stephanie's body that was now lying still on the closet floor.

"She's dead," one of the paramedics announced.

"She's dead. I killed her, "Monica confirmed for the 911 dispatcher that Stephanie was gone. She began to cry. "I killed her!"

The second paramedic worked on Keisha who was still struggling to breath. The investigation revealed ligature marks around her neck. Stephanie had tried to choke the life out of her. Keisha was a survivor and would be okay. Monica had finally put an end to the torture and hell that Stephanie had put the family through for the past fourteen months.

Darius and Jamel arrived one behind the other. Keisha and baby Keyana were both rushed to the hospital. Darius rode in the ambulance with them while Monica stayed behind to talk to the detectives. Jamel remained by her side, consoling her because she was visibly shaken. In his heart, he worried. What was going to happen now? What was Stephanie doing there in the first place? From the looks of her clothing, she came to hurt someone, but it all backfired; thanks to Monica.

They would later find out that Stephanie planned to kill Keisha and kidnap the baby. The police found a car seat in the back of the car. They also found a diary with the details of her plan covering several pages. There was a bag of baby clothes, pampers, blankets, and a few other items in the trunk that she purchased at Target the day before. She was trying to hurt Darius in a way that she knew would be effective. She wanted to destroy his life, his happiness. She knew that he loved Keisha and that hurting her and stealing their baby would destroy him. That would not be happening today, or any other day. It was finally over.

ABOUT THE AUTHOR

Terri Seymore-Green is a native of Southampton, NY. She has worked in the banking and finance industry for more than 23 years, but her true gifts and talents are in writing short stories, poetry, and novels. She holds a Bachelor's degree in Human Resource Management and a MBA. Terri currently lives in a town in Prince George's County, MD. *I Love You More Than Love* is her first published novel, so she would love to find out what you think. She can be reached via email at PoetryandProseII@gmail.com, on her blog at www.PoetryandProseII.com, or you can write to her at Poetry and Prose II, 15912-B Crain Hwy Suite 308, Brandywine, MD 20613.